Jagadish Mohanty (1951–2013) was an influential Odia writer whose most productive years were between the 1970s and the 1990s, although he was active right until his untimely death at the age of sixty-two. A trend setter in Odia short fiction, he mediated the existentialist experience of angst and alienation, thereby giving Odia literature the much needed international exposure. Two finest short story collections out of his thirteen are *Dakshina Duari Ghara* (*South-Facing House*), published in 1979, and *Album* (1981). The two are also available in English translation. He wrote five novels, including *Kanishka Kanishka* (1986), which explored the moral dilemmas faced by ordinary individuals in their quest for an authentic existence. *Nija Nija Panipatha* (1990), translated as *Battles of Our Own*, is a unique Indian example of the industrial novel.

Himansu S. Mohapatra is a literary critic and translator. He has produced, with Paul St-Pierre, an edited volume of Odia stories in English translation, entitled *The Other Side of Reason* (2007), and two fiction translations: *Basanti: Writing the New Woman* (2019)—the first woman-oriented Odia novel written by nine authors in 1931—and *Letters to Jorina* (2021), an epistolary novella by Ganeswar Mishra. A selection of his literary journalism has been published as *Model of the Middle* (2014). He studied at Sambalpur Univerisity, Odisha, and University of East Anglia, Norwich, and taught English at Berhampur University and Utkal University, Odisha.

Paul St-Pierre taught translation in Canada. He has collaborated on translations of literary texts from Odia into English. Among these are: *Six Acres and a Third* (by Phakirmohan Senapati, co-translated with R.S. Mishra, S.P. Mohanty and J.K. Nayak and published by University of California Press: 2005 and Penguin: 2006; a later translation [*Six and a Third Acres*] in collaboration with Leelawati and K.K. Mohapatra was published by Aleph in 2021); *Atmacharita* (also by Phakirmohan Senapati, co-translated with D.R. Pattanaik and B.K. Tripathy and published by National Book Trust of India, 2016). In 2019, Oxford University Press published his co-translation, with Himansu S. Mohapatra, of *Basanti*, and Aleph published *The Greatest Odia Stories Ever Told*, a collection that he co-translated with Leelawati and K.K. Mohapatra.

JAGADISH MOHANTY

Battles of Our Own

Translated from the Odia by Himansu S. Mohapatra
and Paul St-Pierre

PENGUIN BOOKS

An imprint of Penguin Random House

PENGUIN BOOKS

USA | Canada | UK | Ireland | Australia
New Zealand | India | South Africa | China

Penguin Books is part of the Penguin Random House group of companies
whose addresses can be found at global.penguinrandomhouse.com

Published by Penguin Random House India Pvt. Ltd
4th Floor, Capital Tower 1, MG Road,
Gurugram 122 002, Haryana, India

Penguin
Random House
India

First published in Odia as *Nija Nija Panipatha*, 1990
Published in English in Penguin Books by Penguin Random House India 2022

ISBN 9780143451747

Typeset in Bembo Std by Manipal Technologies Limited, Manipal

www.penguin.co.in

We lovingly dedicate this work
to the memory of
the late Jagadish Mohanty (1951-2013)
for having written such a moving, out of the ordinary story . . .

CONTENTS

INTRODUCTION

Himansu S. Mohapatra

Nija Nija Panipatha (1990)—translated as *Battles of Our Own*
and hereafter referred to as such—is one of the five novels[1]
written by Jagadish Mohanty in a long career spanning
half a century during which he emerged as an undisputed
trendsetter in modern Odia literature. The novel stands
out in the author's oeuvre for its gritty realism even as
it displays the best of the existentialist and psychological
veins of his short fiction. Centred on the conflict-ridden
world of a colliery, it is the first undoubted exemplar of an
'industrial novel' in Odia, and, perhaps in Indian literature.
The novel provided him a wider canvas for exploring the
battles within the self and society. The coal mine setting
was ideal for this exploration. The novel is thus set apart
from the majority of mainstream Odia novels of the time,
with their polite and placid settings and their themes of
romance or social success.

A quick detour now to briefly recount the author's life.

II

Mohanty was born on 17 February 1951 in the iron-mining region of Gorumahisani in Mayurbhanj, a tribal-dominated district on the northern periphery of Odisha. After finishing his early education in his hometown, he studied for two years in far-off Belpahar in the west of Odisha, where his elder brother was employed with the Tata Refractories. What precipitated this removal was his father's voluntary retirement from his job and his decision to return to his native village in the district of Singhbhum, in the neighbouring state of then Bihar (now Jharkhand). This was indeed a traumatic dislocation for him.

Mohanty returned to his father's native village after finishing middle school in Belpahar and went to his village high school, passing the school finals with distinction. For some inexplicable reason—probably not unconnected with the prospects of employability—he chose a vocational line and graduated in Pharmacy from SCB Medical College, Cuttack. He landed himself a job as a Pharmacist at the Himgiri Rampur Colliery, the oldest open-cast coal mine in India, in the district of Sambalpur (now Jharsuguda), on the western periphery of Odisha. His entire working life was spent in this colliery. It was here that he lived with his wife Sarojini Sahoo, an acclaimed writer of short stories and novels in her own right. Mohanty died in the nearby industrial town of Belpahar in a freak accident on 29 November 2013 while trying to cross at a level crossing.

This brief account of Mohanty's life is enough to suggest that it was hardly a life ideal or even suitable for a literary career, lived as it was on a perilous industrial, social and cultural borderland. The spectre of industrialism haunted the author throughout. It is then remarkable that, navigating the 'base forcing of the human potential'—the expression is D.H. Lawrence's—he experienced and witnessed around him, he was able to give his heart and soul to writing. He became modern Odia literature's chief 'epicist' of the industrial experience of alienation. He was indeed the stuff that literary lore is made of. In his life he wanted to link Odia literature with the avant-garde currents of European literature. In his death too he became linked with the famous scenes of railroad death depicted in Western fiction, notably Charles Dickens's *Dombey and Son* (1848) and Leo Tolstoy's *Anna Karenina* (1878).

III

Mohanty wrote all his life in isolation from and in defiance of the power and culture capital of Odisha, and he wrote mainly to negate the mainstream literature that was unadventurous, conformist and dull. In a cult short story of the 1970s with the title 'The South Facing House', he shows how the problem of contemporary Odia writing seems to lie in its refusal to allow the exploration of new frontiers. This is highlighted in the short story by a battle of the books and authors. J, the central character, and very much modelled on K of Franz Kafka, asks his girlfriend if she has read Camus. She assumes that she has been asked about Kanhu Charan, short for Kanhu Charan Mohanty (1906-1994), the popular Odia writer of romances and a byword for romantic escapism. Her answer, in a further shocking display of a conventional mind set, is that she has read Bhupen Goswami (1923-1998), a popular writer of Odia detective novels. Mohanty's point clearly was to stress the conformist values of middle-class Odia readers. Accordingly, in his writing he sought to smash and tear down the old edifice of words and to build a new one.

IV

In a sense, *Battles of Our Own* is the most personal of Mohanty's works, though the word 'personal' is not to be understood in an autobiographical sense. Its setting and characters are drawn from the author's long experience of working in a colliery.[2] The personal in Mohanty carries the force of his peripheral or marginal location.

As observed earlier, Mohanty drew on the existentialist literature from Western Europe to breathe fresh air into the often staid, uptight and cloyingly sentimental world of modern Odia literature of the 1970s. This did not deter him from being responsive to the demands of realism, which had been the forte of modern Odia prose fiction from the time of Fakir Mohan Senapati (1843–1918), the architect of the modern Odia novel. The portrayal in *Battles of Our Own* of the stark, gritty industrial underbelly—in Odisha and, by extension, in India—stands testimony to this fact.

Realism and existentialism, however, were not enough to sustain Mohanty, who in the 1990s woke up to the pressing issue of moral commitment, to the need for conscientious objection in a social and political culture rendered hopelessly corrupt and compromised. The novel was thus the site of the author's ideological struggle, his own 'Panipatha'[3] or 'Kurukshetra', to use the word in the title of the 2015 Hindi translation of the novel.[4] The existentialist hero (Pradyumna) of the novel yielded first place to the Gandhian hero (Harishankar). The ideational world of the industrial novel with its triangular contest among Marx (power), Kafka (angst) and Gandhi (conscience) gravitated towards Gandhi.[5]

V

Set in a colliery, *Battles of Our Own* sets out to show the world of the coal mine from up close and below. The significance of this can be realized by its attempted reversal of Milton's classic view in *Paradise Lost* (1667) of 'bands of pioneers rifling the bowels of the earth and digging out ribs of gold'.[6] Mohanty's bottoms-up view, an inversion of the pioneers' view from above, show us the actual process of this coal—or black gold, one might say—extraction which involves, not engineers, but miners who work underground, putting their lives on the line. These are the loaders, coolies, dressers, trammers, and waggoners that the novel presents from up close.

The achievement of the novel is to make this dark underworld graphically visible. There is no dearth of suspense and action in this fast-paced narrative, punctuated with face-offs between the workers' union and management, jealousies among officers, fiery speeches, fights between rival trade unions, based on opposing ideologies of Marx and Gandhi. Never before in Odia fiction has a novel delineated so memorably the gloomy, soot-blackened, and conflict-torn human environment that has come to be known as industrial. If it brings to mind the Bollywood blockbuster *Kaala Patthar* (dir. Yash Chopra, 1979) in terms of setting, it also lets itself be seen as a realistic counterpoint to the celluloid fantasy in terms of theme and characters. The following lines early on in the opening chapter of the novel are revealing, commenting as they do on the contrast between the reel and the real:

> Before he had ever seen an actual coal mine Pradyumna had imagined it would be like in a film, with a lift to take miners down. When he had seen the coal mine here he had been disappointed: there wasn't a pulley or a lift, just a long tunnel and a flight of stairs after the cave-like entrance. At the bottom of the stairs was the principal haulage track, and from that point began the nether world. (Chapter 1)

VI

The narrative traces two parallel stories. The first is the story of the deracinated middle-class youth, Pradyumna. Caught in the throes of the transition from the countryside to the industrial town, he moves from his ancestral Brahminical village near the coastal town of Puri to the coal mine at Tarbahar on the western fringes of Odisha. Ironically, however, he can get a job only by impersonating a tribal.

This might fly in the face of common sense, but it is something that was rooted in fact. In an email letter (dated 1 November 2013) to this writer the author explained the real-life circumstances that gave rise to such cases of impersonation. The collieries and coal mines were set up in the mineral-rich forested areas of the western periphery, home to the native tribal population. The tribals faced large-scale displacement, as a result. As compensation the government offered jobs in the colliery to the hill men who lost their land, obviously the lowest that were available. Here the infamous coal mafia stepped in to take advantage of the situation. They paid those hill men who were offered jobs a small sum of money—big to them because they were so poor—which they were duped into accepting. These jobs were then sold for huge sums of money to non-tribals who were in need of jobs. It goes without saying that the mafia were hand in glove with the colliery authorities, the corrupt politicians, and trade union leaders in arranging such fixes. In *Battles of Our Own* this nexus is emphasized through the bitter fight over gaining control of the trade union of Tarbahar Colliery.

Pradyumna is one such beneficiary of the racket run by the coal mafia, although he is a reluctant impersonator. As Samaru Khadia on the employment rolls and as Pradyumna Mishra in the intimate and informal sphere, he leads a dual life, becoming the focus of the existentialist concerns that permeate the novel. Ironically, however, he can return to being Pradyumna Mishra only by selling himself to management. This he does, but this means for him the substitution of one form of inauthentic existence for another. He redeems himself by deciding to quit his job and get out of the sordid world of the colliery altogether. He does, however, become the reader's peephole into the underbelly of the colliery, with its atmospheric gloom as well as its moral vacuum. Mohanty captures this in a beautiful passage in the opening chapter that sets the tone of the narrative:

> The world down below was completely different, dingy, dimly lit and sordid. The tubs ran along the haulage tracks; from somewhere would come the boom of an explosion, and the earth would shake. Black shadows ran every which way. The light attached to the headgear cast shadows over people's faces, enveloping much of them in darkness. (Chapter 1)

VII

The second narrative, the moral heart of the novel, centres on Harishankar Patnaik, the erstwhile secretary of the trade union. He has suffered reverses in his career after falling out of favour with the local MLA, now an influential minister in the state. As a result, he has lost the position of secretary of the union to his younger and unscrupulous rival, Dhruba Khatua, for whom unionism is pure business. The Gandhian values of Harishankar have been made obsolete and redundant in the new dispensation—the colliery serves as a microcosm of the post-independence comprador national culture—based on greed for money and lust for power. At the novel's opening he has withdrawn from political life, minding the family he had long neglected and rearing a fawn or rather burying it after its death from being bitten by dogs.

This narrative then traces the events leading to Harishankar being pulled out, albeit unwillingly, of his seclusion. It focuses on his efforts to form an alternative union based on the Gandhian virtues of non-violence and satyagraha, his desertion by his fellow workers through the manoeuvring of a shrewd, calculating management, his pressing on with the hunger strike, and his eventual death. The long last chapter in which Harishankar alternately retrospects and hallucinates provides a tragic closure to the story. The message of this second narrative, as of the whole novel, is clear: Harishankar must redeem a life scarred by compromises, half-truths and prevarications by a Gandhian act of satyagraha, even if it ends in self-annihilation and a sort of pyrrhic moral victory.

Harishankar's narrative is also the reader's window into the tricks and stratagems of the colliery administration to push for profit and production. The administrators themselves are stripped of humanity in the process. Deshmukh, an upwardly mobile officer, is a prime example of this reduced humanity in the novel. There are many instances of this dehumanisation in the narrative, but what stands out is Deshmukh's loveless marriage with Anita. His inability to perform as an effective manager is echoed in his sexual paralysis. The bedroom is his most daunting 'Panipatha': he and Anita cannot make love. Mohanty adds an extra layer of complication to Deshmukh's personality by showing him as trapped between his mother's possessive love and Anita's proprietary wifely demands.

Mohanty, like Dickens in his industrial novel *Hard Times* (1854), is ultimately unable to imagine trade unionism beyond the opposing extremes of opportunism (Dhruba Khatua) and self-sacrificing idealism (Harishankar). He does, however, provide a resolution to the conflict at the heart of the industrial world by emphasising the inevitability of moral choice. Harishankar's saving grace, as the novel takes pains to show, is his idealism, which makes him a better human being than opportunism can ever produce. In his life he practices the austerity and simplicity of a Gandhi. In his death-defying fast he is a steadfast Gandhian. *Battles of Our Own* fittingly closes on this final image of tragic heroism. An ageing man fasting unto death on a mat, in his last bid to seek absolution for the sins of his selfish brothers as well as manipulative masters, is a master stroke.

> But now it seemed to him that Gandhianism was the most valued path; there was no other way to proceed. He believed in it firmly. A strong moral force was taking control of Harishankar, forcing him not to call off his strike. (Chapter 16)

It is at this point when he sheds his prevarication that Harishankar grows in moral stature, eclipsing both his unionist allies and his management adversaries.

VIII

Finally, the novel's human concern—highlighted in an industrial novel's intriguing psychological sounding title— with the individual psyches of each of the main battle-scarred characters, Harishankar, Pradyumna and Deshmukh, is its foremost value. Every one of them has a history of personal trauma arising out of poverty, desertion and marginalization. These are all characters that have received a raw deal from their respective family and environment, and, stand alone on the battlefield of life. The parallel between two characters on either side of the social divide is worth noticing. Deshmukh is a high-level officer in the colliery and Harishankar Patnaik is a down-at-the-heels working class leader. But they are alike in their feeling of vulnerability in the face of larger impersonal forces. With a true novelist's gift Mohanty has individualized them, thus rendering them complex and immune to stereotyping.

Harishankar, the eldest son of a tottering family, is left to bear the burden of the family from an early age, when his father becomes a sanyasi and walks away. He can never get over this, especially the final memory of his father wading deeper and deeper into the desolate fields, leaving him, a young boy, stranded on the edge of the village at a twilight hour. Harishankar's desertion by his father is matched by the young Deshmukh's excommunication along with his mother, by his family and community in far-off Jalna, in Maharashtra, after his father's death. He too is haunted by the deep psychic wound this ostracism has caused. He tries unsuccessfully to get over it by being ruthlessly upwardly mobile and paying dearly for this with his increased servility to the system. On top of all this is the guilt he feels—again matching Harishankar in the guilty feeling he harbours for being an unworthy son—for not doing right by his mother, who had braved the entire world in order to make a man of Deshmukh.

Pradyumna too has his share of psychic scars. Unable to do well in life and love, constantly subject to insults and slurs, forced to change his identity to make ends meet, he is the archetypal loser, the prototypical 'unheroic hero' of modern fiction. He does not have a future with Minakshi, the woman he loves. Nor can he marry Jhunu, the young girl he meets in the colliery, despite the sexual tumble he had with her once.

With the acuity of perception characteristic of a sensitive novelist, Mohanty renders a twisted world. It is a world in which the illicit has become licit. In such a world the last vestiges of a dwindling humanity are preserved in characters that are, in their respective spheres, the left out or the ones standing in the last row. In *Battles of Our Own* Mohanty draws on social realism, psychoanalysis and existentialism to deliver a complete experience of the 'industrial novel' in Indian literature. The act of rendering this novel into English has afforded me and my collaborator[7] the pleasure and opportunity of a translational descent into a literary region not often visited, and, in the process, Mohanty's *Nija Nija Panipatha* has happily morphed into *Battles of Our Own*.

Notes

1   The other four novels are *Kanishka Kanishka* (1986), *Durdina* (Bad Days, 1998), *Uttaradhikar* (The Inheritance, 1998), and *Adrushya Sakala* (The Invisible Morning, 2004). None of these has been translated. Mohanty authored thirteen volumes of short stories.
    Two are available in English translation: *South-Facing House and Other Stories* (Black Eagle Books, 2020) and *Album and Other Stories* (Authorspress, 2019), both translated by Karunakar Mohapatra.
2   The main characters of *Battles of Our Own* are widely believed to have been based on real-life persons in Himgiri Rampur Colliery, where Mohanty worked as a pharmacist. So close

are the portraits to their real-life counterparts that a case can be made for reading *Nija Nija Panipatha* as a roman-à-clef.

3   Incidentally, 'Panipatha' or 'Panipat', as historians refer to it, is the name of the historic battlefield in north India associated with the dawning of Moghul rule in Delhi in 1526, the year in which Babur, the Moghul chieftain from Kabul, defeated the Emperor of Delhi, Ibrahim Lodi, and replaced him as Emperor. Thereafter, two other historic battles were fought at Panipatha, between Akbar and Hemu in 1556, and, between the Maratha and the Durrani Empire in 1761. In the novel, 'Panipatha' functions as a metaphor of both outer and inner battles.

4   *Apna-Apna Kurukshetra*, translated by Dinesh Kumar Mali; Delhi: Yash Publications, 2015.

5   It was in the course of my aimless wandering through the newly started Bhubaneswar book fair in 1994 that I happened upon a copy of the Odia novel by Jagadish Mohanty at a bookstall for Odia books and bought it. The book was quickly read; but it did lie in limbo for a good two decades before being reborn in my perception as a defining work. It helped me discover the roots of my alienation and world-weariness in my inherited middle-class dilemma over moral and political commitment, mirrored in Pradyumna's existentialist stasis. And then later the novel took on a whole new meaning, being seen through the perspective of its second lead character, Harishankar, the working-class leader. He, the true protagonist in my opinion, seemed an invitation to move beyond the existentialist stasis of Pradyumna and of other alienated characters through an act of conscientious commitment, an act of faith, which in this instance was Gandhian. At a time when we have entered the 152nd year of the birth of Gandhi, having reached a milestone at the 150th

year, no other novel in the modern Odia corpus seemed more worthwhile to be showcased through translation. *Battles of Our Own* is the fruit of that desire.

6   John Milton, *Paradise Lost*, Book 1, Line 687–90. *The Norton Anthology of English Literature*, Vol. 1, Sixth Edition, edited by M.H. Abrams. New York: W.W. Norton & Company, 1993, p. 1492.

7   The 1990s were also the decade in which I met up with Paul St-Pierre, who is my collaborator on this translation. He was a Professor of Translation at Montreal University, Canada. Work involving translation had brought him to Odisha, and once the initial project was finished, he moved on to new ones with new collaborators. The visits have continued and so have the translations, which number now over forty. This includes our conjoint translation of the first collaborative novel in Odia, *Basanti*, recently published as *Basanti*: *Writing the New Woman*.

BATTLES OF OUR OWN

ONE

Why did everything seem coated in grime? The tables and chairs, the office of the timekeepers, the lamp cabin, the electrical room where the batteries were charging, the tin roof overhead, the shed on one side—almost everything was in its proper place. Yet, dingy and bathed in gloom.

The door to the lamp cabin on the left; on the right, the timekeepers' counter. For a coal miner there was no choice but to check in with the timekeeper, who would be bent over one ledger or another. He would hand over a slip, to be taken to the lamp cabin, where it would be produced and exchanged for a lamp and a battery. The moment the lamp was attached to your helmet, and the battery shoved into its holder at your waist, you were transformed into a coal miner. This was exactly what happened to Pradyumna in this novel.

Down in the coal mine he was not known as Pradyumna Mishra, but as Samaru Khadia, the son of Baithu Khadia, an illiterate member of a scheduled tribe. Above ground he returned to his original identity, to being Pradyumna Mishra once again, the son of retired schoolteacher Sri

3

Sarbeswar Mishra, from the Brahminical village of Puri. His family at home included, in addition to his parents, his educated sisters of marriageable age; and his married but out-of-work elder brother, his brother's wife, and their five-year-old daughter. Once, when the timekeeper, bent over the form filled out by those going down into the pit, had asked Pradyumna his name, he had come close to blurting out his real one. Immediately he had cut himself short. It dawned on him that every time he came to the pithead his identity changed.

Beyond the machines charging the batteries there was a small opening. This was the main entrance to the mine, where a man—the body checker—was stationed. He frisked the miners going down for bidis, cigarettes, or matches.

Before he had ever seen an actual coal mine Pradyumna had imagined it would be like in a film, with a lift to take miners down. When he had seen the coal mine here he had been disappointed: there wasn't a pulley or a lift, just a long tunnel and a flight of stairs after a cave-like entrance. At the bottom of the stairs was the principal haulage track, and from that point began the nether world. Someone with the name Pradyumna Mishra would have been out of place there; Samaru Khadia took over from him, and his designation changed to 'casual loader'. At first, the foreman had given him loading work. It paid good money, but the work was hard. Pradyumna could not manage it, and so his uncle, a regular at the union office, had put in a word with the manager and got him the job of tub checker.

Being a tub checker was a bit like being a babu. Timbermen, or dressers, or haulage trammers, or waggoners, or tub riders were labourers and got covered in coal dust. A tub checker, though, only had to keep track of what the tubs brought in and took out. And it meant an extra rupee or two per tub in addition to your salary. What better job could there have been?

After he started working at the mine, Pradyumna lost another illusion he had formed from films and storybooks, about the poverty and exploitation associated with coal mining. There were no signs of that anywhere; people had enough money. Another form of deprivation did exist, though: they didn't know how to spend the money they earned. No one had upgraded from string cots to comfortable beds; the houses didn't have curtains on the doors or windows; the wives, even of miners who earned two thousand rupees a month, did not have decent saris. This had left Pradyumna perplexed.

Of late, however, he had ceased to wonder about all this. He had grown accustomed to the coal mine that at the beginning had shocked and surprised him. When he had first arrived at the colliery house of Agani Hota, a relation of his from his village, Uncle Agani had touched his hand to his head, and exclaimed, 'Have you gone mad? Do you think it doesn't cost money to get a job in a coal mine? For the job of a loader on shift duty there're people with BAs and MAs lining up; they have to pretend to be illiterate to get their names registered. Not only that, but to jump the line for an interview costs five hundred or a thousand rupees paid under the table to the man at the Employment Exchange, and then you have to grease the palm of the labour officer, or of the personnel officer. If you get through that, then you have to cough up more money for the medical-fitness certificate. If you have a hydrocele or an eye problem you're done for. The doctorbabu will ask you for two or three thousand rupees for the certificate. There's no chance of ending up with the job in a hurry.'

Pradyumna was well aware his uncle and aunt were not pleased with the way he had landed up at their house out of the blue. He had seen them speaking in hushed tones behind his back, going quiet when he was present. He had wanted to leave, but the thought of returning home made him feel utterly helpless. Why was that? Why?

Uncle Agani had asked him: 'What's missing at Sarbeswar Bhaina's house that you want to work in a godforsaken place such as this?'

Pradyumna's father was by no means rich, but he was comfortably off. As far as others were concerned, he was well off indeed, probably because he had a house with an asbestos roof and a cement floor. In addition, he had two ponds, fifty to sixty coconut trees, five or six acres of land, and a pukka house in Balagandi Sahi in Puri, which had been rented out.

But all of this was what outsiders saw. Pradyumna knew that in reality the situation was not so good. His three unmarried sisters sat at home with nothing to do, after passing their MA degrees. No marriage prospects were in sight. The older brother did not have a job, but he wouldn't leave the village or farm the land. He had a wife and daughter. In the house, along with Pradyumna and his parents, there were two labourers, four pairs of bullocks, two cows that gave milk only for the three months after they calved, a maidservant, and a twelve-year-old boy who ran errands. That such a large family could not manage on the paddy from six acres of land, the produce of fifty coconut trees, and the rent on their house in Puri—this, Pradyumna knew all too well.

According to his sisters, Pradyumna was selfish and lazy. His sister-in-law considered him a burden on the family, only thinking of filling his belly. His father had once thought he had a bright future, but when Pradyumna failed his BA degree he concluded Pradyumna would follow in the footsteps of his older brother. This made Pradyumna unhappy. As for his friends, they tended to sideline him because he was sickly and weak.

Requests and demands to do chores and run errands— from his parents, his brother and sister-in-law, and his older sisters—inundated him as soon as he returned home. 'Ruku, I told you to get my sari cleaned.' 'Ruku, you didn't post the letter today, did you? The deadline's tomorrow for the application to reach Bhubaneswar, and it won't get there if it isn't sent today.' 'Ruku, you didn't get me cigarettes at the market, did you?' 'Ruku, Halia, the labourer, has gone to Sakhigopal with three hundred coconuts—haven't you followed him to check the rate he's selling them at?' 'Ruku, sugar's sold out at the fair price shop—you didn't let us know.' 'Uncle, my literature textbook's available in the market; will you get it for me?' Pradyumna found all this too much. The market was a mile and a half from his village, and he had to take his bicycle to get there. No matter how hard he tried, he could never manage to satisfy everyone, nor could he understand why everything was made to seem so urgent.

Ever since his childhood Pradyumna had been all skin and bones; his clothes rarely fit. His hair was thin and brittle. All of which explained why he was shy in front of strangers. His mouth would go dry when people talked to him; he was afraid they might not pay attention to him because of his size. He would become confused, and feel acutely embarrassed.

Everyone seemed to ignore him. Shopkeepers would continue on with their business instead of attending to him; serving boys at eateries would hover around his table, without bringing the food he had ordered; bus conductors addressed him familiarly using 'tume' or 'tu' instead of the deferential 'apana'. All of this left him feeling slighted.

His friends and acquaintances also gave him the cold shoulder; his health made him the butt of their jokes. It never occurred to them that he was made of flesh and blood, that he too had feelings, that he could feel hurt and humiliated. His opinion never carried any weight. Pradyumna was only twenty-one at the time. After he failed his BA, everyone began asking him what he would do next, and suggesting that he ought to do something.

Whenever his married elder sister was home on a visit she would berate him. 'Ruku, is father getting any younger?

There're three sisters at home still waiting to get married, and you can see for yourself your older brother's good for nothing. The money from the land isn't enough for a family this large. Is father strong enough to take care of things? What are you planning to do? Are you going to start a business or get a job?'

His unmarried middle sister would chime in. 'Ruku's such a loafer that business would be beyond him. That takes someone with wit and intelligence. He's only fit for a ten-to-five job.'

His sister-in-law would add: 'If you sleep until ten every morning, Ruku, you won't be fit for either business or a job.'

And then his younger sister: 'Ruku won't even go and put a letter in the post for you. In his hands, not even a sprig of spinach will cook.'

One day even his father heaved a deep sigh. 'I expected Ruku would turn into something', he said, 'but in the end he's as useless as his older brother. That's called destiny. One suffers like this only if one is destined to.'

Pradyumna had felt deeply hurt that day and been on the verge of tears. He had wanted to go to his father and say: 'I'm only twenty-one years old. Yes, I failed my BA. All my friends are still studying, at universities and colleges. They're fooling around, enjoying themselves. You people wanted me to start earning a living at such a young age. You might have thought I'd do an MA or an MPhil before going out to look for a job, you people were in such a hurry.'

Lying on the string cot in a room in the small two-roomed, asbestos-roofed house his uncle had in the colliery, Pradyumna overheard the hushed conversations between Uncle Agani and his wife. That was when he decided how he would act in the coming days.

The Pradyumna who had never set foot in the kitchen while in his village, who had never scooped out a glass of water from the handi, busied himself in the kitchen the following day in an attempt to win over his aunt. He took over all the chores: lighting the wide-mouthed coal oven, typical of the colliery, after filling it the night before; washing the clothes; making roti; tempering the dal and seasoning the curry; shopping for vegetables at the weekly market. He had been surprised to find he had so much strength and enthusiasm, he who even one trip to the vegetable market near the bus stand would drain of every ounce of energy and cause him to snap at anyone who wanted him to go back on another errand. Things were so different here!

The world down below was completely different, dingy, dimly lit, and sordid. The tubs trundled along the haulage tracks. From somewhere would come the boom of an explosion, and the earth would shake. Black shadows ran every which way. The light attached to the headgear, cast shadows over people's faces, enveloping much of them in darkness. In the beginning it had been difficult for Pradyumna to identify people underground; all the faces looked the same. These days he had got used to the darkness and was able to make out shapes and figure out passages.

The office of the tub checkers was near the conveyor belt. Two empty wooden boxes that had housed explosives served as a table and a stump of wood as a chair. A bare light bulb burned overhead. Two or three grimy registers were piled on the table. When he looked for Ananta, the tub checker of Relay A, Pradyumna did not find him. A new man had replaced him, and he did not bother with Pradyumna, staying bowed over his register doing his calculations.

Pradyumna was not sure if Ananta had left for good and this new man was now in charge, or if this was only a temporary replacement because Ananta had missed the last shift. Pradyumna stopped for a moment. 'Are you on A shift?' he asked.

Without looking up the man answered in an offhand manner. 'B shift.'

'I'm supposed to be working on B shift. Who the hell are you? What's your job? Why are you sitting here?' asked Pradyumna.

This time the man lifted his head, his look as hard as stone, as if he was ready for a fight. 'The foreman told me to work as a tub checker starting today. My position is general labourer; I'm a permanent worker. Anything else you want to know? Go and ask the foreman. Now, let me get back to work.'

Pradyumna's ears reddened from the humiliation. Most of the people from the colliery were rude like this, unable to say anything in a civil manner. People here always behaved impolitely.

He had got the position of tub checker only because Uncle Agani had used his influence with the manager. So how could this have happened? What if the foreman had transferred him to the loading section? Loading the tubs was very hard work; loaders came out of the mine with aching shoulders and backs. Pradyumna shuddered at the thought of going back to loading. He would not be able to work that hard; not only that, but being a loader was no better than being a labourer.

Pradyumna knew no one in the mine could comprehend why he was feeling so helpless. The foreman who sat out there giving out the jobs would never be able to understand that a boy from a Brahmin village, who had failed his BA, had never dug a shovelful of earth or harvested an ear of paddy, let alone held a ploughshare. Only someone in Pradyumna's place could understand how pathetic it would be for such a boy to load coal into a tub.

Still, Pradyumna went to see the foreman. There was a mob around him, of the typical country people and labourers from the coal-mining area. They all wore torn shorts or dirty lungis, with a belt and batteries. Their vests were pitch black and filthy, their helmets covered with dirt and grease. The foreman seemed to lord it over them. It was said he was illiterate and had been employed as a loader when the Company had run the mine. With great difficulty he had learned to sign his name. The inner reaches of Pradyumna's mind were clouded in anguish at the thought of having to curry the favour of this ignorant man.

Pradyumna remained standing. Once the rush was over, the foreman looked at him and asked, 'Hey! Why aren't you working? What's your name?'

Pradyumna almost gave his real name, but checked himself just in time. 'Samaru Khadia', he said, 'casual loader.'

The foreman looked at his notebook. 'Okay', he said. 'Go and do loading. There's been an explosion in sector six on level five. Bhimsen Bairagi's your partner. Go and load your tub.' Pradyumna protested. 'But I've been signed up as a tub checker.'

The foreman laughed, a sarcastic uncivilized laugh. He made fun of Pradyumna. 'Signed up as a tub checker, have you? So what? As if you were born a tub checker. Bloody casual loader. You'll have to work your guts out in whatever job you're given. You'll bloody well have to. Says he signed up as a tub checker!'

Pradyumna gritted his teeth so as not to say anything after this earful. Before starting to work he'd been very sensitive, taking to heart his friends' jokes, his sisters' reprimands, and his father's rebukes. He would sulk for days. After that, he had come to accept them. These sorts of comments were commonplace, and it would be hard to survive if he gave them any weight.

Pradyumna came back out of the pit. Not saying anything to the foreman, he told the timekeeper, 'Put me down as a no-show today.' The timekeeper looked up. 'Name?' he asked.

'Samaru Khadia. Casual loader.'

'Why a no-show?'

The timekeeper asked the question automatically, without expecting an answer. He pored over the register to find the name of Samaru Khadia. Pradyumna said nothing. He returned his lamp at the counter and left.

What he saw demoralized him: the heaps of coal at the entrance to the mine, the conveyor, the wagons and the trucks. This was a lonely coal mine in a tiny place away from any town, and an even lonelier residential colony. His destiny was tied to this place; the dreams of his college days had been abandoned. Once he had had hopes of being important, of rising to an important position, but now he seemed destined to spend the next thirty or forty years of his life exiled in this lonely land, under an assumed name and identity. That he was the son of Sarbeswar Mishra, from the Brahminical village of Puri, that he had studied at S.C.S. College—all this would become a lie and he would live his life as Samaru Khadia, the son of Baithu Khadia, a scheduled tribal. He would be deprived of any hope for achievement or success. He would be like everyone else in this coal mine, coming to the pit in the morning and returning home at dusk, dog tired. Except for holidays, his days would form one continuous blur.

Pradyumna was devastated. When he fondly looked back over the twenty long years he had carefully built up his identity he almost broke down from a sense of despair. He was intensely aware that he had no friends, that he was alone with no one with whom he could share his feelings of isolation, his burdens, or who could comfort him with a soft hand on his back.

TWO

Three men were digging, perspiring profusely. Harishankar's fifteen-year-old son, his second, was seated a short distance away, overseeing the work. Harishankar himself sat on the roots of a tree stump, exhausted. He stared blankly at the sky. Near his feet lay the carcass of a young deer.

What was the time? Harishankar had forgotten to wear his watch. The sky had been cloudy and misty since morning. It was already afternoon, he guessed; two, maybe four o'clock. The fawn had died earlier that day perhaps, and a few hours had passed.

Harishankar stretched out his hand and gently stroked the animal. Even now its back felt soft, like velvet. His second son had wanted to skin it, but Harishankar had told him off in no uncertain terms. It seemed horribly cruel to remove the skin, even if the animal was dead—like skinning one's own dead son.

Controlling his emotions had always been a problem for Harishankar. His political guru, Hemanta Babu, had drummed into him right from his youth the simple lesson that if you went into politics you had to give up all feelings and emotions, had to be practical and look out for yourself, that the only interest in politics was self-interest.

Harishankar knew full well that Hemanta Babu's advice was based on knowledge of the world. When he had turned fifty, he had begun to realize his senses had become numb. In the past trivial things would make him very emotional; now they didn't even provoke a reaction.

And yet how flat and empty the world seemed now that the fawn was dead! Something that had been here, that had existed, had ceased to be. At his age small pains and joys ought not to affect him. Why was this different?

He had brought the deer home a year ago. Someone had caught the three- or four-month-old animal in the jungle near Rairakhol and sold it to Harishankar for one hundred rupees. It would feed only on milk then; much later it learned to eat grass. Harishankar had weaned it himself.

Its golden skin was covered with white and dark spots. Its innocent eyes seemed to look at the scenes around it in wide-eyed wonder. At the beginning it was nervous and would jump and hop about as if caught in an earthquake; its feet would slip from beneath it as soon as they were planted on the ground. It would panic at the sight of people, and leap about in a frenzy. But it knew Harishankar well, approaching him and brushing its muzzle against him like a motherless child, cuddling up to its father in search of affection.

After going into politics Harishankar had lived in a stupor and felt neither love nor attachment. He had a twenty-five-year relationship with the trade union in the coal mine. He had first become involved in union activities for the benefit of the workers, to prevent them from being exploited by the owners.

Once familiar with trade-union activities he realized the unity of the downtrodden and the struggle against exploitation were mere illusions and did not correspond to the realities of life in trade unions. In fact, trade unions were a form of politics, and politics was nothing but excitement and intoxication.

The three men kept digging. They had already been at it for a long time, but there was still more to do. How much more? How large a hole did it take to bury a fawn? Harishankar stroked it one last time. So young and innocent! It had come, leaving its mother behind in some far-off deep forest. What had it wanted from Harishankar? Security, in the form of two fistfuls of grass twice a day? Happiness, in a full pot of milk. Had these needs been met?

The fawn could easily go into a sulk. Once it had stayed away from Harishankar for two days after he had slapped it in anger. That day he had been shocked to discover that animals, like humans, had feelings, felt love, passion, and anger. His second son had named it 'Jali', after the deer in the well-known Odia story by Kalindi Charan Panigrahi, 'The Lament of the Flesh'. He was in the habit of saying that all that was needed was a dog named 'Dora'. Harishankar had answered in jest: 'One day a Sahib will come, kill the fawn, and eat it.'

Harishankar knew very well that, not even the General Manager, let alone high-level officials in the colliery, like the

Deputy Chief Mining Engineer and the Manager, would dare hurt a fawn that was the pet of an ex-secretary of the trade union. Harishankar had always thought of himself as a person whose opinions carried a certain weight; he had certainly considered himself important when he was the secretary. But there was something far more important and that was the passage of time. Time, in fact, was as powerful and as brutal as the white Sahibs.

Suddenly Harishankar felt the sight of the fawn being buried would be too much to bear. It was best to leave. Once he had decided this, he stood up and told his son: 'You people see to the burial; I'm going.'

He said this and made his exit. The road ahead descended from the ridge in a long downward run, with his house at the bottom. His second son was in the habit of calling his house 'the garden of peace'. With walls of stone and earth, a tiled roof, and a courtyard with a well, it was on the border between the colliery and the residential colony. His eldest son, who worked as a bank officer in Hyderabad, had once asked: 'Papa, why did you build the house in such a wretched spot?'

Harishankar had never planned to build a house. After Hema Babu became a minister, he placed a piece of vacant government land in Harishankar's name as a gift. Giving him five thousand rupees, he told Harishankar: 'Go ahead and build your home, Harishankar. You've never done anything for yourself.'

That day Harishankar was overcome with gratitude. He told his eldest son, who had nothing but disdain for Hema Babu: 'See how much Hema Babu cares for me?'

His son was dismissive. 'Cares for you? He bought a luxury hotel in Bangalore after becoming a minister. And a Toyota car. And built a bungalow in Bhubaneswar. Not to mention the gold jewellery for his second wife, all the money in the bank, and the black money stashed away in foreign accounts. What did he give you? A piece of unused government land and five thousand rupees!'

Harishankar had not yet been thrown out of the trade union in disgrace. He was full of admiration for Hema Babu and of no mind to understand what was so terrible about Hema Babu taking bribes and increasing his wealth. Until then Hema Babu had seemed very close to his heart. Harishankar felt he had some kind of a right to Hema Babu's property.

Harishankar came out of his reverie when he heard someone greeting him. He raised his head and saw Giridhari standing before him obsequiously. Giridhari had started an eatery in the station bazaar. Earlier, when he had first come to the area, he had been dirt poor, selling vegetables on a pushcart. A little later, he rented a shed and set up a betel shop. Then came the eatery and now he owned a two-storied house in the heart of the market area. On top of all that there was talk of the good money he was making on the side from the tickets to films shown on his video machine. Giridhari said: 'Heard the fawn was dead. It was very nice.'

Harishankar did not respond. Giridhari would not have come all this way just to express his grief for the death of a fawn, unless there was some other motive. In particular, he would not have taken the trouble of heading up towards the ridge when he did not find Harishankar at home.

Giridhari asked, showing respect, 'How did it die?'

'Bitten to death by stray dogs.'

'Aah!' Giridhari made a sound expressing sorrow. 'These innocent animals create attachments. I know from personal experience that deer and parrots are the two creatures that do not last very long. My grandpa used to keep deer as pets, but not a single one survived. They died by flinging themselves against something while leaping about, or falling, or getting torn up on the barbed wire.'

Harishankar took his place in the front yard of his house. His mother sat leaning against the wall. While looking up at the sky, she addressed Harishankar. 'Did you bury the fawn? The children from the neighbourhood came by asking if they could buy it. Do people eat the flesh of a dead fawn? I had no idea. Besides, since it was bitten by dogs, its flesh must be poisoned. The children were saying they would share the meat. I told them you had taken it out to bury it. Their spirits sank at the mention of your name and they gave up.'

Harishankar said nothing. He called out to his youngest son. 'Go and see if there's any chance of getting some tea.'

'Why tea, Sir? I've just had some', said Giridhari, once again respectfully.

'That's fine. What's wrong with some more? Sitting on his tin chair Harishankar looked off into the distance. On the ridge the three diggers and Runa seemed to disappear into the mist. What were they doing? Hadn't they finished digging the hole? Weren't they done burying the fawn?

Giridhari remarked as soon as he saw the front yard. 'When did you have the well dug? Will you put a cement circle around it? Or will you have it walled inside, using cement rings? You've got to do one or the other, or else the dirty water from the ridge will seep into the well when it rains.'

Just then Harishankar was wondering if he should have buried the fawn himself. It seemed to him as if the four people were digging on the ridge to bury his youngest son, Kuna, and not a deer. The next moment he realized what he had been thinking. God, how inauspicious!

Giridhari continued. 'You finally got around to building a house, but not a good pukka one. Despite your long years as the secretary of the union, you made nothing for yourself. Look at Dhruba Babu. See how he was able to buy a motorbike after only six or seven months as secretary. When you left your post there were twenty-two thousand rupees in the union's coffers, but there's not even a paisa now. Eighteen thousand rupees are owed the central committee, but haven't been paid. There are no funds.'

How was Giridhari up on so much? Harishankar knew he was very clever. He was the kind of fair-weather person who always made sure to protect himself with an umbrella when the weather turned foul. Once Hema Babu lost the election when his first wife went to court, questioning the legality of his second marriage. Hema Babu lost the village-council election. He was an object of vilification everywhere. The management of the colliery had completely ignored him. At the time Giridhari's

eatery had a 'pay when able to' register for those from
the union who wanted to pay later. He used to supply tea
and tiffin to the union people when they sat around and
chatted. Hema Babu stayed in the colliery and did not go
to his home in the nearby village. That house belonged to
his first wife. Nor did he and his second wife ever meet.
She was in Berhampur, where she was a lecturer. It was
only after bearing him a daughter that she found out about
the existence of the first wife and her ownership of all his
property. When Hema Babu was in midst of this crisis,
Giridhari had called out to Harishankar one day: 'I can't
manage any longer, Harishankar Babu. How can I run
my eatery if bills aren't paid for months? And it's not just
the bills owed by the union. Do you know how bad it is
for the reputation of my eatery when an immoral person
like Hema Babu frequents it? Decent people have almost
stopped coming. I can't let this go on any longer. Please,
Harishankar Babu, take your discussions elsewhere and
leave me alone.'

From that day Harishankar had not liked Giridhari. The
same person was now sitting in front of him. 'I met Hema
Babu on my trip to Bhubaneswar', he said.

Harishankar had been right that there was some reason
behind Giridhari's visit. Talking about Hema Babu was only
a way to lay the ground for the real subject. But what could
that be? What was he really interested in? Harishankar tried
to guess, but to no avail.

'Hema Babu was saying, this Hari fellow's terribly
self-centred. No sooner did I make Dhruba secretary of the

union so he could strengthen it than Hari kept his distance and took offence.'

'Took offence, did you say? I've never ever done or said anything against Hema Babu.'

'Don't I know this? Let Hema Babu say what he will, the fact remains nobody thinks beyond his own self-interest. He even went so far as to say Harishankar would not do well to challenge him. I asked what he meant by that, what he was planning on doing. I told him plainly Hari Babu was the sole reason he became a minister. I asked him if he were to return to his constituency tomorrow, would he be able to win without Hari Babu's support?'

Harishankar knew Giridhari was lying. He must never have spoken these words to Hema Babu. On the contrary, Giridhari would have behaved obsequiously and been only too happy to malign him. Harishankar only laughed to show his disapproval but did not say anything.

'Hema Babu went on, "What haven't I done for Harishankar and what has he done for me in return? Can he be so selfish as to turn away from me for something as trivial as a mere secretary's post?"'

Trivial? Harishankar began to boil inside. He felt as though the person seated before him was not Giridhari but Hema Babu himself. How dare he say depriving him of the secretary's post was something trivial? For him the position was not a road to other things. He had never thought of capitalizing on it in order to become the chairman of a municipality or a secretary or executive member of the ruling party in the village or the state. He had not thought of using his position to give his own people jobs in the colliery. He had not increased his bank balance or built a bungalow. These were the things that were trivial. He could have done all that; he knew how to go about it. Yet he had abstained from it. Why? Because the union was not just a mere formality for him, and certainly not a rung on an upwards ladder. The union was his dream. For twenty-five years he had poured all his strength and vigour into it, spending his blood and tears. Did anyone know his wife had gone mad? And why had that happened? He had become so involved in union activities he had not been able to give her the love and companionship she needed and deserved. Except for his oldest, the rest of his sons had become wayward. Why? Because they had been brought up in his aunt's house and not given the love and attention that was their due. As a father he had not done his duty by them. He had given up his wife, children, family—nearly everything—for the sake of the union. It had taken precedence because it had been formed against heavy odds. They had struggled hard to keep it alive and healthy. Before the nationalization of the industries the owners of the collieries had regarded union members as enemies. Circumstances changed afterwards. Then, the leaders of the union were shown respect by the owners. The role they had been cast in under the private companies changed. They went from being rebels to being kings; but once that happened, they started to sell out the union, the living monument to their dreams, sacrifices, and success, and he had lost out as everyone scrambled to fill their own selfish needs. The union was taken away from him. No, it was not due to some external force. There were divisions within the union and Hema Babu had appeared on the scene in the role of an arbiter. He took the post of secretary away from Harishankar and gave it to a person like Dhruba Khatua, who until then had been a junior member with nothing but his unscrupulousness to recommend him. Why hadn't Hema Babu done this twenty-five years earlier? If he had, then Harishankar's wife would not have gone mad and his children would not have turned out so badly. He could have been happy in the role of an ordinary family man.

Harishankar returned to the present. It was Giridhari who was standing in front of him, not Hema Babu. 'You failed to understand Hema Babu', he was saying, 'but I knew what he was really like. He belongs to no one. He eats the tip of the tree branch he sits on. Anyway, let it be, Harishankar Babu, now you have to pull yourself together. You have to show Hema Babu who you are and what you're made of. I heard in Bhubaneswar that Hema Babu was backing Dwivedi in the upcoming election for municipal chairman. Just tell me what bloody qualifications does that Bihari have? Other than owning a liquor shop? Can he boast of sacrifice, of seniority? Can anyone be made chairman simply because a minister wants him to be? I've thought of running for chairman myself. Will you give me your support, Harishankar Babu? Of course, I'll only enter the race if I have your blessings.'

Now Harishankar understood why Giridhari had suddenly appeared, fawning over him. 'No, Giridhari

Babu', he answered. 'I'm no longer involved in politics. Please don't drag me into this.'

'What on earth are you saying, Sir? You've given up on politics? Out of fear of Hema Babu? You've no idea how powerful you are and how much support you have. You have to simply be strong and step out, and you'll see the mantle of leadership slip off Hema Babu.'

'I'm just an ordinary person, Giridhari Babu. I know how incapable I am. I'm completely unfit for politics. Had I dived into it earlier, I would probably have gone further than Hema Babu long ago. With my own eyes I've seen the many ups and downs of his political career. There was a time when he was falling so rapidly that I had to haul him up, holding him by hand. The thing is that for the past twenty-five years I was living in a dream. Once it shattered I find I'm just an ordinary human being, only a stock verifier in the general manager's office.'

Kuna came in, bringing two cups of tea. It was tasty, with not too much sugar. Harishankar remembered his mother had told him a few times already they were out of sugar. Where did she get sugar from? One of the neighbours?

'Please think about it, Harishankar Babu. It won't do any good if you allow yourself to cave in so quickly. Politics is like wrestling. Change the hold a bit and tighten or loosen your grip and you'll end up with your back on the ground.'

Harishankar looked off into the distance. What had the four men on the ridge been up to for so long? How deep was the hole? Had they finished? Would the soul of the fawn sulk because Harishankar had not been at the burial, just as, when it was alive, it had sulked and kept away after being slapped? Harishankar peered into the mist and could make out four black shadows. What had they been up to for so long? What time could it be?

THREE

Once out of the mine Pradyumna went to the hospital for a medical certificate.

'What's wrong?' the doctor asked.

'My belly aches.'

The doctor felt his stomach. 'How are your bowel movements?'

'Regular.'

'Your name?'

What should he answer? He knew he could not give his real name; his whole being had been shrunk to the dimensions of Samaru Khadia, the very existence of Pradyumna Mishra had been denied, his college days and over twenty years of life as Pradyumna Mishra had been betrayed. Sadness engulfed him.

Pradyumna obtained the certificate. With it he could apply for leave on the grounds that he was not able to work, but he was not entitled to sick leave. This would count as leave without pay. Once he had left the hospital he threw away the medicine that had been prescribed. It was Samaru Khadia who had a stomach ache, not Pradyumna Mishra.

At least that was what the hospital record said. In the end, Pradyumna guessed, the reason why his uncle had bought him an Employment Exchange card on the black market was due in part to his aunt's suggestion and in part to the prospect of having Pradyumna in the house and being able to help her out. On that day he had told Pradyumna, 'Look here my boy, if you try to get a job through regular channels it'll take at least four or five years before you're called to an interview. What's more, there's no guarantee you'll be selected or offered the job even once you are. First, you'll have to queue up in a lungi at the Employment Exchange office to get your name registered. And then there're certain conditions to be met: you have to be from the locality, illiterate, and a resident of the Notified Area Council ward.' Money was important, and for that reason alone Pradyumna had taken on the role of a tribal youth, in denial of who he really was.

When his uncle had first suggested the change in identity Pradyumna had not been willing. After all he was a Brahmin; he had studied up to BA level. It would be a blow to his self-esteem to work as an illiterate tribal youth named Samaru Khadia.

Here is how things would happen. 'A false certificate would be obtained from a member or from the chairman of the Panchayat after greasing some palms. Then it would take some more money for the people at the employment exchange to comply and arrange for an interview letter. To get through the ordeal of the interview top officials at the coal mine would have to be bribed and asked for special favours. After that, an application would have to be put in to the tehsildar for a certificate of residence, and a court fee of one-and-a-half rupees paid. The tehsildar would then refer the matter to the Revenue Inspector, who would also have to be appeased. He would certify the existence of landed property amounting to X number of acres and decimals in such and such locality of such and such a block which, it would be specified, is within five kilometres of the coal mine. The medical check-up would take place only after taking care of refreshments for everyone in the tehsildar's office, from the nazir to the peon. For a clean bill of health money would have to be paid to the doctor, under the table. It's all a money game, my friend. Far easier is the other way of doing things: paying two thousand rupees for an interview card. The group or party it's bought from makes all the arrangements to get you over the hurdles, from the interview to the certificate of residence to the medical fitness certificate. Then you don't have to stop here, there and everywhere to grease the palm of all and sundry.'

This was an alien world for Pradyumna. He had no previous acquaintance with its ways, manner, and morals, and was not in a position to understand what the best way of doing things was. All the same, he had strong reservations about paying two thousand rupees for an interview letter in the name of Samaru Khadia. After all, he was Pradyumna Mishra, the son of retired headmaster Sarbeswar Mishra, and college-educated.

Uncle Agani grew tired of explaining things to him. What's your objection, he would ask. No one by the name of Samaru Khadia will come and challenge you. Besides, what's the value of an education these days? Lots of MAs are becoming loaders. Think of yourself as an actor, cast in the role of Samaru Khadia, his uncle would tell him. Think of the colliery as a stage where playing Samaru Khadia will get you two or three thousand rupees a month, he would say. Many people take up acting for the sake of a square meal. There's no cheaper way of finding a job in a coal mine. Do it if you want to; otherwise, forget about it and go back home.

The thought of returning to his village depressed Pradyumna deeply. Before his eyes flashed pictures of his jobless days in the village, of the three-kilometre cycle ride to the market with his friends as he tried to hide his feelings of inferiority. The bitter memories of his sisters calling him lazy and selfish, the abuse heaped on him by his father, his mother's deep sighs and his sister-in-law's ironic smile as she handed him tea—all these kept Pradyumna from returning to his former life. But consider how strong that old life's claim was on Pradyumna Mishra, on his existence. Wasn't his mind still resisting the translation of Pradyumna into Samaru Khadia? Pradyumna, of course, had accepted the life of Samaru Khadia because he had been forced to do that. And so you see, money was indeed all important!

Pradyumna stood up. Where to now? If he went back to Uncle Agani's house, he could bathe and freshen up. But he didn't feel like doing that. If his aunt set eyes on him she would make him run some errands. But then there was no other option. He could not go anywhere until he had changed out of the dirty shorts and shirt he wore to work. The very thought of his uncle's house brought to mind a prison. It was totally uncivilized. Most of the people in this colliery lived such lives, with little or no sense of decorum.

After arriving at this place he heard rumours. Agani uncle had had a vasectomy at the time of the Emergency, pressured by the authorities after having two daughters. Despite this, a son had been born only five years ago. His younger daughter was outgoing and loose in character, in the habit of hanging out with young boys. Pradyumna also heard she would sometimes go off with one or another of her boyfriends for nights on end. The elder daughter was withdrawn, with no interest in anything except her own little world. There was also a Christian boy, who was very close to the family, and of whom she was very fond. The extent of her obsession with him was enough to make even the most liberal-minded person wince.

Uncle Agani had two bad habits to go with his many good ones. One was returning home drunk every evening, and the second was frequenting his Chhattisgarhi concubine in the slums of this mining area. At times, when auntie got angry with him, she would shout at the top of her voice, 'Why don't you go live with your Chhattisgarhi wife?'

For Pradyumna, such quarrels in front of their two grown-up daughters were out of place. But then it amazed him no end that his uncle never ever asked his auntie about the mystery of her youngest son's birth. No matter how drunk or angry he was, he never taunted her about it. He deeply loved his son Sonu.

Pradyumna had never imagined he would find himself stuck in such a family. His uncle used to go to his village occasionally, spending lavishly while he was there. His coal mine job brought him lots of money, and everyone in the village eyed him with wonder and appreciation. Before leaving the village Pradyumna had harboured weirdly romantic notions about life in the coal mine and about his uncle; when he arrived there, he received a huge shock.

Pradyumna noticed that his uncle's way of life was very much the rule rather than the exception. Life in the colony was rife with salacious gossip—so and so had eloped with someone's wife; a man was keeping two or three wives; a woman of forty-five was making off with a nineteen-year-old, leaving her grown-up sons and daughters; and so on. Pradyumna came from a coastal village of Brahmins. No one in his family observed austere caste rituals or performed priestly duties, yet as Brahmins they were imbued with a subtle sense of the superiority of their caste. This held them prisoners to social conventions. Otherwise, he would have been able to be open with his father about his relationship with Minakshi. But this had not been possible. His three sisters were still unmarried. If he married a woman from another caste, what would their future be like?

'You only thought about your sisters, Pradyumna; you never cared about what would happen to me.'

Pradyumna suddenly remembered the face of Minakshi Balabantray, the daughter of Kulamani Babu, who worked in the District Judicial Magistrate's Court in Puri and who rented the house his family owned in Balagandi Sahi. He

pictured her raising her head, which had been buried in
the pillow a moment before. Her eyes were red, swollen,
and full of tears; her hair was dishevelled. She was clad in a
kota sari that had been highly starched and had sharp creases
from the heavy iron. She sniffled as she said, 'You weren't
a child when you fell in love with me and kissed me for
the first time; when you wrote to me, asking me to go to
a movie with you in secret; when, surrounded by Bengali
tourists on the sea beach, you encouraged me to dream.
You were an adult and knew the ways of the world. Didn't
you know then that I was from the Khandayat caste, that
my father was an ordinary clerk, that I was two or three
years older than you, that you were from a Brahmin family
and had three sisters still to marry off? Didn't you know
how important maintaining the status quo was for you? So
tell me why you came forward? How can I offer these lips
to someone else when I've already offered them to you?'

Pradyumna had felt helpless. Did he really love
Minakshi? What was the nature of his love? In Puri he had
felt a tremendous attraction to her, but back in his village
he had felt he should forget her. After moving to the coal-
mining area he realized he would never be able to bring
her there nor would she be able to cope. That only made
Minakshi seem all the more precious and their flirtation the
stuff of sweet memories.

Pradyumna returned to Uncle Agani's. He saw the
younger daughter, Jhunu, in conversation with two boys
on the raised platform surrounding the neem tree in front of
the house. One of the boys was seated on a bicycle and the

other was standing with a foot on the platform. The people around were eyeing them with curiosity. Jhunu of course paid no attention to this.

Pradyumna went inside. He took off the plastic helmet, as if removing a heavy burden. Setting it on the table he sat down on a metal chair and started to untie his laces. Housing in the mining area was pathetically inadequate. There were two rooms, each eight feet by nine, with an asbestos roof, a veranda at the back where the cooking was done, a tub with water below it, and a platform for bathing. The courtyard was not too large, and a wire was strung across it to hang out clothes to dry. It contained a guava tree. The toilet and the storage place for coal were at the back. The surprising thing was that such a tiny house could accommodate so many people. It was jammed full of things. There was a trunk under the cot, and under the beds in the two rooms were a box, a broken wooden crate, Runu and Jhunu's used and tattered books, shoes, bits of electric wire, and a fused tube light. A string bed with a steel frame was folded up against a wall in the front room. A black-and-white television was placed on an old rickety table. On the shelf on the inside wall were steel utensils, a container filled with vermillion, bangles, powder, cream, hairclips, and a hanging mirror. The décor and furnishings were very lower-middle class.

By comparison Pradyumna's house in the village was more refined and elegant, thanks perhaps to his sisters, who were all well-educated and had a sense of taste. They had given their tiled house a sophisticated look. Pradyumna did not really understand what his own house had that was missing in his uncle's, but while the former exuded a sense of completeness the latter seemed impoverished. This despite the wealth of his uncle, compared to whom his own father earned nothing.

Pradyumna stopped in his tracks as he was going into the bedroom. Uncle Agani's elder daughter, Runu, and her Christian friend were lying on the bed. There was nothing offensive about their posture, but they were lying together on the same bed. Perhaps they had been busy gossiping before Pradyumna came into the room. Now Runu lay with her back to Peter, her friend, who was poring over a Hindi magazine.

Runu acted coy before Pradyumna; she did not speak to him. Her back was turned to him. Peter did not mind being seen by Pradyumna. Without any qualms he lay there unconcerned, his eyes glued to the magazine. The scene shocked Pradyumna. But why? Because of his conservative attitude? Suddenly, he thought of Minakshi. He would not have been able to lie with her on the same bed like this. Their love was not platonic, though of course he had not yet made love to her. Minakshi was not the kind of girl to go to bed with a man before marriage.

The passage to the courtyard went through the bedroom. Pradyumna moved towards it. He made his way to the water tub adjacent to the cement platform. Dipping his hand into the water, he sat there for some time, lost in thought. He knew his uncle was thinking of marrying his elder daughter to him. Pradyumna ought to feel grateful to his uncle for having got him this job. Should he have become angry at what he had seen in the bedroom? Would Minakshi still be waiting for him?

A long heavy sigh escaped his lips. Life was indeed strange. Whose life was it anyway? Pradyumna Mishra's or Samaru Khadia's? Who was he really? Pradyumna or Samaru? Was life worth living at all? His mind was enveloped in gloom.

FOUR

Deshmukh did not feel any calmer, even after two pegs of whisky. Was the alcohol even having any effect? Normally two pegs were enough. If he drank more, he would feel light-headed. Sometimes even sick.

Anita must have gone out. Had she come back yet? A short while ago, as she was setting out the ice cubes, soda, and bottle of whisky, the maid had told him there was a meeting of the ladies club that evening. Anita did go out quite a lot. And so she should! What sort of life was possible in the officers' colony of this coal mine? If Deshmukh found life boring, despite his work at the mine, his projects, and the office, how much more monotonous things must be for Anita, confined as she usually was to the four walls of the house.

Deshmukh emptied the second glass of whisky despite himself. Somehow he did not feel anything. Another peg? He had instructed the maid not to bring any visitors straight into the room, especially not Anita's lady friends. The door was closed, but not bolted. What time was it? National programming must have begun on television. Should he move to the drawing room?

Anita's absence made the house feel lonely and empty. His daughter, Bucchu, was in class eight at the central school. Where was she at the moment? Studying or sitting in front of the television? Or out with her mother? Anita had insisted he stay away from Bucchu if he had been drinking.

The bungalow seemed deserted; Deshmukh felt very alone. The maid was probably doing something in the kitchen. Deshmukh was in the small storeroom, seated in his easy chair, his feet up on a stool, surrounded by the discarded old biscuit and ghee tins, trunks, wooden boxes, the piled-up curtain made of the roots of fragrant grass, the discarded air cooler, and Bucchu's broken bicycle. Should he have one more peg?

Anita was very proud that her husband was sub-area manager, an E-4 level executive due for promotion to E-5. He was the supreme authority on the coal production unit at Tarbahar Colliery. As a senior executive, he was right after the general manager and two or three deputy chief mining engineers and staff officers in seniority. He learnt from Anita that the E-1, E-2 level executives and the wives of doctors and engineers eyed her jealously. Deshmukh had also heard her stories about the pecking order at the meetings of the ladies club, where women were seated according to their husbands' designations. He had also got to know the intimate details of the officers' lives, household expenses, and the behaviour of their wives towards their servants and maids.

But did Anita understand Deshmukh was nothing more than a helpless hapless slave? Did she know how poorly he had been treated by Mr Mishra, the deputy chief mining engineer? Did she know about the humiliating scolding Deshmukh had received from him? Perhaps he would have been happier as an ordinary loader or clerk; then he would not have been answerable to or have had to be loyal to anyone. And, above all, he would not need to worry about comments on his private conduct.

He thought back on the tongue-lashing he had received from Mr Mishra, provoked, or so it would seem, by Anita's supposed lack of courtesy towards his wife. Because no formal invitation had been extended to the ladies club, Anita had put forward a resolution at its executive meeting to boycott the eye-operation camp sponsored by the Rotary Club. What's more, during the last eye camp wives of the Rotarians had reportedly misbehaved towards members of the ladies club. Deshmukh was himself a Rotarian, unlike many of the husbands whose wives belonged to the ladies club.

Anita was the secretary of the ladies club. The wife of the deputy chief mining engineer was the vice president, and the wife of the general manager was the president. The resolution, of which Mrs Mishra did not approve, was adopted at a meeting of the executive body in her absence. How would he explain this to Mr Mishra? After all, he was a responsible Rotarian and the eye-operation centre had more or less been set up at his initiative.

Deshmukh knew that it was solely a ladies' matter and it was not wise to get involved. But Mr Mishra had got it into his head that Deshmukh had arranged for his wife to propose the resolution in order to insult him. Would it be proper for Deshmukh to ask Anita to change it? No, he could not pressurize Anita for such a trivial thing. That would amount to acknowledging his powerlessness, a way of making public his subservience to Mr Mishra.

'Huh! The deputy chief mining engineer is your boss, not mine. Why do I have to greet him?'

Anita had not said namaskar to Mr Mishra when she met him at a party for the first time and had got angry when Deshmukh had pointed out her faux pas. From that day forward, the deputy chief mining engineer had fallen in her estimation. In her opinion he had no personality, and seemed to leer at all the women he met. He was under his wife's thumb; he was hen-pecked.

Deshmukh could not understand why Mr Mishra took so much interest in the ladies' affairs. Mr Mishra had given him a dressing down in his office for one full hour earlier that day. The peon had been present throughout, and Mr Mishra had used harsh language with him in the presence of Gupta, the labour officer, Rungta, the clerk, and Mahapatra, the steno. Deshmukh had tried to defend himself, but to no avail.

Deshmukh poured himself another peg. This was his last bottle. Had he gone through his monthly quota? Why were his stocks depleted; it was only the twentieth of the month. Anita would not want him to spend more on liquor. His budget was two hundred rupees a month, and Anita was always on the alert, making sure it did not exceed that.

Besides, Bucchu was growing up and starting to understand things. Deshmukh stayed away from her when he had been drinking, and Bucchu, for her part, also learned to avoid him on those occasions.

Deshmukh felt restless. There was no sign of Anita's return from her outing. Where had she gone? The maid was busy in the kitchen. Bucchu and Deshmukh each pretended to ignore the other's presence. The large house felt very empty. Deshmukh went outside. The cold was deepening its hold. He asked the maid to bring him his sweater. He was not feeling well. Today Mr Mishra had given him a good chiding. Would he tell Anita? No, he wouldn't, he couldn't. Let the image Anita had of Deshmukh stay as it was. Let her continue to think of him as the monarch of the Tarbahar mining area. Well, let her.

Would he go for a walk and get some fresh air? Or take the car out of the garage? No, too much trouble. It would be hard to find where Anita had put the car keys. Moreover, the engine would refuse to start. Would he call the telephone exchange and ask for jeep number 5498 to be sent to him? Who was the driver on duty today? Ram Avtar or Kalidas?

Jeep number 5498 was reserved for Deshmukh's use. It was old and had earlier been Mr Mishra's. When two new jeeps were acquired, Mr Mishra had claimed one for himself and given the other to Mr Ghosh, the manager–superintendent of mines at the Chingidiguda Incline Colliery.

'Why this rotten old jeep for you? A new jeep for Mr Mishra and a new one for Mr Ghosh, but for you the old 5498?'

Deshmukh had not given Anita any quarter then and had shut her up. 'Don't meddle in official matters! You're a woman, so behave like one', he had said. Fine, he had shut Anita up, but Mr Mishra's behaviour had hurt him all the same.

The telephone was in the drawing room. Bucchu was there, watching television. Would he go across to the drawing room? Would she be able to smell the alcohol? It was as if he thought Bucchu knew nothing about her father's drinking. She did know, and was getting wiser by the day. He ought to keep himself under control. Things should not be allowed to come to a point where Bucchu would start hating her father because he drank too much.

Deshmukh did not go to the drawing room, but into the front garden. Where had Anita gone? Why was she taking so long? The moon had not yet risen. Why weren't the streetlights on? Which electrician was in charge of the area? He would have to tell off the electrical engineer in charge of the workshop tomorrow.

Deshmukh stood in the dark. He was from a small town called Jalna, in the Marathwada region of Maharashtra. His childhood and adolescence had been spent among the backward and uneducated inhabitants of that town. He had not seen any place larger than Aurangabad until he passed his matriculation examination. He knew nothing about politics, of whichever variety: Shiv Sena, Dalit Panthers, or Congress. At Marathwada University he had been a brilliant student.

Standing there in the dark, Deshmukh had the feeling his life had gone off the tracks. This dirty and godforsaken

Tarbahar Colliery was not the place for him. Right from his matriculation day he had dreamt of Mumbai, but had been unable to spend a month there, let alone a whole year. Had he wasted his life? Should he have lived elsewhere and differently? Where and how? Would Mumbai have been the answer? Would it have brought in as much money and a car? He felt sad and depressed. It seemed to him he would not flinch if he were to meet Death itself at this very moment. On the contrary, he would embrace Death without a qualm, as if he were going to sleep.

The venom-spewing face of Mr Mishra made its way into his consciousness. What if he were to shoot that henpecked man in the back? His reverie broke the next moment, and he thought: Oh, no, he had drunk too much today; he had to control himself more from now on.

FIVE

It had been a long time since Harishankar had gone to the general manager's office. Whenever he went, he would sign the attendance register for fourteen days at one go. As the secretary of the union, he had remained absent from the office for months on end. The clerk in charge of wages would hand them over without checking the register. These days Harishankar needed to come to the office at least once a month, preferably a few days before salaries were being prepared.

When Harishankar had been the secretary no one had complained about his irregular office hours, but now he could clearly sense there was discontent over his absenteeism. As it was, most of the staff in the general manager's office was given to taking things easy, arriving late and leaving early, sometimes in the middle of the day. But Harishankar was the greatest shirker of them all; for months he did not go to the office. The finance manager, his immediate boss, did not make an issue of this. Moreover, the general manager, who knew the value of diplomacy in managing industrial

affairs, knew how important it was to keep on the good side
of the secretary of the workers' union.

But now that he was no longer the secretary,
Harishankar felt sidelined. Earlier, not merely the labourers,
but also the staff in the general manager's office, would
come to him with their petitions: a loan that had not come
through, a complaint about not being given a promotion,
two increments that had not been sanctioned, a grievance
about not being allotted official quarters. Harishankar knew
only too well he could not help any of them, but everyone
believed it was within his power to do so. Now that he
was no longer the secretary no one came to him. He had
suddenly become a nobody. Everyone gave him the cold
shoulder; he had been pushed into a solitary existence. He
had no work. He didn't have to try to get somebody's order
of dismissal cancelled, or find somebody's brother or son a
job, or enter into serious discussions with the deputy chief
mining engineer or the general manager about whether a
loader should fill two carts or four each day.

After signing the attendance register Harishankar looked
in the direction of the finance manager's office. He had not
yet come in. Only two or three of the clerks had shown up.
It was eleven o'clock. Since Harishankar had not come to
the office for a long time, he was unaware of its unwritten
schedule. Ghosh Babu, a second-grade accounts clerk, said:
'Hello Netaji. Did the sun rise in the west today? How
come you've shown up?'

Was he being sarcastic? Had that Ghosh fellow placed
stress on the word 'Netaji'? Was he hinting at the fact

Harishankar was no longer the secretary? Harishankar did not answer. How this poor Ghosh had kowtowed to him to be promoted from third grade to the second! Look at him now, taunting him and smiling ironically!

Harishankar left the finance section. One corner of the corridor had been partitioned off, and a tea stall set up. Two thousand rupees had been sanctioned for entertaining guests, and used for the tea stall. It supplied free tea to everyone's guests and friends in the general manager's office, from the big boss himself down to the peon.

After he became the secretary, Harishankar had objected to the practice. The personnel officer had told him: 'Harishankar Babu, government property is up for grabs, and lakhs of rupees are being misappropriated by the deputy chief mining engineer, the sub-area manager, and the project officer for "projects". Here we're only drinking a couple of thousand rupees worth of tea. How can life go on if there's a fuss over such trifles?'

Afterwards, Harishankar had realized the personnel officer was right. He had been carrying with him the idealistic legacy instilled into him twenty-five years earlier when he had first entered trade-union politics. He had been caught up in a romantic dream of emancipating innocent workers from the exploitation of mill owners through class struggle. Years of experience had taught him how absurd that dream was. A trade union was like a business: one had to lead a double life; one had to be pro-worker in front of the workers, but always ready to give in to management, as if one's very existence depended on their kind attention.

Harishankar understood no one can engage in trade-union politics without the blessings of management. The kind of union politics involving fights with management and adopting adversarial stances was no longer relevant. Labourers wanted their immediate needs met and their grievances settled. Only if you could take up such causes—fighting against dismissals, suspensions, and transfers, or helping fellow workers secure a loan, or getting a job in the company for somebody's son—only then would you qualify for the title of 'Netaji'. It was precisely for these reasons you needed the goodwill and co-operation of management. Battling for it in the Labour Court and in the real world outside was never going to make it possible to attain these ends.

After the personnel officer's comment Harishankar stopped protesting against the unauthorized tea stall. He knew a union leader could not bring about change, whether for better or for worse.

He went over to the tea stall and asked Ram Dayal, the peon in charge, for a cup of tea. Ram Dayal turned to Janaki, seated nearby, 'Give the babu a cup of tea', he said.

Ram Dayal did not stand up. Janaki was sitting on the floor, leaning against the pillar. She did not budge an inch when she saw Harishankar, let alone greet him respectfully. She said to Ram Dayal, 'Hey, why don't you get it yourself?'

Had Harishankar been reduced to nothing more than an ex-union secretary? Had he been stripped of everything else: personality, self-esteem, the dignity connected to his job, personal relations? Janaki's husband had been a foreman. After his death in the mine Harishankar had done a lot of running around to get her the unpaid wages, to get the helpless woman a job, and, above all, to get her posted in the general manager's office as a general worker. This person, who at that time had made a great show of humility and gratitude, always drawing attention to her helplessness, this person who had always been begging for pity—did she care only about Harishankar's official title and not about him as a person? How else to explain the disrespect Ram Dayal and Janaki were treating him with now? On a different day, they would have been very prompt to express their grievances and would have affected extreme friendliness and warmth.

Harishankar felt very sad, as if he did not exist as a human being. He heaved a deep sigh. Ram Dayal was pouring tea into a cup, but Harishankar had lost interest in tea. He decided to leave and was just going past the personnel office when Bala Mukunda, the general manager's peon, came to him. 'Sahib's been wanting to meet you for the last three days. He's in his office now. Please go in and see him.'

So, the general manager had been looking for Harishankar for the past three days. The thought made Harishankar uneasy. His day of misfortune had come. Was Mr Mirchandani annoyed with him for being absent from office? Mr Mirchandani had taken up the position of the general manager just as Harishankar was leaving his position as secretary of the union. They had met only a few times, and these days Harishankar was rarely called to meetings. He did not feel comfortable about making a point by introducing himself, although he knew such discretion had no place in politics. You had to put on a show of not giving a damn about what people thought no matter whether anyone cared to believe you or not. Your words always had to exude power, strength, and might. If you kept a low profile, no one would give you the time of day.

Harishankar knew this was a flaw in his character. He knew he was congenitally incapable of bravado. He regarded boastful talk as trickery, and always behaved with humility and deference. Once when Hema Babu was secretary, when the collieries had not yet been nationalized, there had been a strike at Tarbahar Colliery that had led to a lockout. Even during those critical times Harishankar would greet the officers respectfully whenever he met them.

Harishankar paused for a moment before entering the general manager's office. Might he be angry with Harishankar? If he was that would clearly indicate their relationship was of a subordinate to a superior. Should he try to test the waters by first having a word with Mr Mahapatra, Mr Mirchandani's personal assistant? Harishankar found himself in an awkward situation. The peon was not around to announce him. He had to push the door open himself. 'May I come in, sir?'

The general manager looked up. 'Oh, Harishankar Babu? Please come in. I've been looking all over for you.'

Harishankar felt relieved; so the general manager was not cross. He moved forward, his feet on the soft carpet. The room was refreshingly cool. Mr Mirchandani was seated on the other side of a huge desk. He was an E-8 level officer, soon to move up to E-9. Rumour had it he was going to be made the next executive director. Harishankar sat down.

Graphs and charts relating to production in the colliery were hung on the wall behind the desk. The air cooler to his right was running smoothly, barely perceptibly. Harishankar was suddenly filled with happiness. He had not had a meeting with such a high-ranking officer in a very long time.

Ringing the call bell the general manager summoned his peon, telling him to bring two cups of tea. 'So, Harishankar Babu', he asked, 'how's life in politics going?'

'Don't you know, sir? Hema Babu had me expelled from the union?'

'You may feel badly about that, Harishankar Babu, but let me tell you this: Hema Babu isn't a good man. He thinks only of himself. Consider this: he has had many things done through my good offices, but once in Bhubaneswar, when I met him in relation to some personal work he could have gotten done in a jiffy, simply by making a call, he wasn't at all forthcoming. But then that same Hema Babu has gotten so much done through me.'

Harishankar looked down. Who knew Hema Babu better than he did? All the same, he still felt uneasy when someone spoke ill of him. Was this the result of having been loyal to him for so long?

'I heard you gave up on politics after getting the sack from Hema Babu. Why are you making such a huge mistake? No one gets a free ride in politics. You have to ride roughshod over others.'

Harishankar sighed deeply. 'I've thought about it a lot, sir. To engage in union politics one needs a godfather. I don't have the backing of either management or Hema Babu's influence as a minister. How could I survive? What resources do I have to face the management, the police, and the labour-union leaders who are opposed to me? Will the police or management protect my volunteers when they are collecting dues on payday? What sort of politics can I do without the support of local management?

Mr Mirchandani answered, smiling. 'That's why I wanted to speak to you. I need you to look after the affairs of Tarbahar Colliery. What's the name of that drunkard who's been installed there as secretary by Hema Babu? Ah yes, Dhruba. I can't understand why our project officer, Mr Mishra, is pampering that man so much. Just look at him, the secretary of a union and yet he's in an alcoholic haze twenty-four hours a day. He seems to have one mission in life: forcibly collecting money from labourers and then squandering it. You'll get all the support you need from the management. I can guarantee that. I'm going to meet the sub-divisional police officer in a couple of days. In the course of our discussions I'll ask him to tell the circle inspector not to bother you.'

Harishankar's feet were visible under the table; the straps of his sandals were coming apart. His dhoti was dirty. Harishankar had never been the kind of person to keep his clothes tidy and clean. They were always dirty. Earlier he had been of the opinion looks contributed far less to a person's image than did inner confidence. Now, he observed that people of the younger generation, and, especially people like Dhruba Khatua, who were ten or fifteen years his junior, gave far more importance to looks and cared much less about inner strength.

Harishankar's mind strayed while listening to the general manager. He was neither a believer nor disbeliever, but was he seeing the result of some major change in the position of his planetary, star, and zodiac signs? For the past few days people with different intentions had been trying to persuade him to return to the union. Was this also the wish of the Great Mover of the Universe?

The general manager continued. 'You should form a separate union. And write to the central committee that yours is the genuine one. Raise your voice against the local management. Speak out about the corruption of our project officer and deputy chief mining engineer, Mr Mishra, at your meetings. If possible, arrange a shutdown of Tarbahar Colliery for a day or two. I assure you I won't implement the seven-day pay-cut rule for that strike.'

Harishankar was taken aback. What was Mr Mirchandani saying? From the day he entered politics he had never ever been asked by a sub-area manager, let alone a general manager, to call a strike. But what was Mr Mirchandani, the general manager and an E-8 level officer, due to be promoted to executive director shortly, saying?

Mr Mirchandani smiled. 'Don't be shocked. You must be thinking: what's this man raving on about. Look here, Harishankar Babu, politics is not a game only for you people; we too are in it all the time. Mr Mishra, the deputy chief mining engineer, is a headache for us. You want to get rid of Dhruba Babu, and I want to get rid of Mr Mishra. So let's join hands and work together. The deputy chief mining engineer is always creating problems for Deshmukh, the sub-area manager. You can consider Deshmukh your own man. Tell him if you need help. What I want is a stir against Mr Mishra, a strong reaction.'

Harishankar now understood perfectly well why Mr Mirchandani had called for him. The general manager had an axe to grind with Mr Mishra and wanted to use Harishankar as his instrument. He closed his eyes for a few minutes. Would he accept the proposal? What harm was there in doing so? Would he once again take on the burden of union politics, with all the stress that involved? But how was life any better outside the union? This was his chance: the general manager was providing the backup, Deshmukh was ready to co-operate. This was the right time indeed. Should he take advantage of it? Should he accept the offer? Why not, what harm would there be in that?

'Okay, sir; anything can be done if you give your blessings', he said. 'The circle inspector of the police station here is new; he doesn't know me. Of course, I have tried to get in touch with him, but do put in a word to the sub-divisional police officer.'

Harishankar left the general manager's room. He had been asked to form a new union. The members of the old executive body had settled peacefully into their office duties and domestic chores after leaving politics. A couple of the old members had joined the new union led by Dhruba

Khatua. In his mind, Harishankar made an imaginary list including some and excluding others. He tried to remember who was competent and work-oriented, but also who was eager for recognition or good at collecting money.

He would have to get a new receipt book printed. The central committee of their old union had split into rival factions, one controlled by Choubeji and the other by Tiwariji, both members of Lok Sabha and from the same political party. This had happened at the time Harishankar was the secretary. Hema Babu had thrown in his lot with Choubeji, and even though Tiwariji had come running from Dhanbad a few times his efforts had not borne fruit. Hema Babu and Choubeji were closer allies politically.

Would it benefit Harishankar to obtain the backing of the Tiwari faction of the central committee by currying favour with its leader? He tried not to think whether it would be appropriate to go down on bended knee before Tiwariji for this. That was what was expected in the game of politics. He needed whatever support was available.

In the meantime, there was a lot of work to do. He had to go and see Deshmukh. He needed to strategize and obtain the approval of the central committee. The old union office was now occupied by Dhruba, so a new one had to be found, along with new furniture and stationery. He also needed to find a few strongmen the size of bulls to collect the dues.

Harishankar felt exhausted at the thought of how much there was to do. He was getting old and was clearly not as enthusiastic as he once had been. Sadness and fatigue were threatening to engulf him. Time was running out; he was in the twilight of his life. Harishankar had never thought about this before; he had put feelings and emotions aside. Hema Babu had always said it was important to keep such things at a distance.

His mind was made up now: he had to make use of the opportunity the general manager was giving him. He would use the general manager, before the general manager could use him. Harishankar's fight was not with a nobody like Dhruba Khatua, nor with Mr Mishra or even Choubeji. His fight was not against exploitation; it was neither for nor against the unity of the workers. His real fight was with Hema Babu, to avenge his humiliation and assert his identity.

But who would come forward to help? Would his old friends be there for him now? Once a man had given up union activities and returned to the role of a householder in the family courtyard, once he had become an ordinary worker, he did not want to remember earlier adventures. Perhaps this had happened to many of his old friends, and he could not count on them anymore. But who would find new men and instil a new spirit into them? For the work he had to do he needed a group, a team. Only if five or six people stood with him would he be able to rebuild the union.

Harishankar was looking through the newspaper at the tea stall in front of the general manager's office. He was unable to concentrate, feeling restless after the interview with Mr Mirchandani. The newspaper was right before his eyes but it went unread. It had become a chessboard on which he was moving his soldiers, infantry, kings, ministers, elephants, and horses.

As he looked up from the newspaper, his gaze fell on Agani Hota, who was standing in front of the eatery. He knew Agani, an electrician at Tarbahar Colliery. He was a spirited man, a member of the old union. He had been kicked out by Dhruba Khatua, but Harishankar knew Agani still went to the union office. His enthusiasm had not been dampened. Dhruba was not giving him any prominence, so he could be brought in. He was enterprising and experienced in the ways of the union. Mentally choosing this electrician, Agani Hota, for the post of assistant secretary in the new union, Harishankar stepped out of the tea stall and put his hand on Agani's shoulder.

Agani turned around and greeted him warmly. 'I came to seek you out', he said. 'Been looking for you for three days.'

'That makes two of us, Agani.'

'I have a nephew. Not a blood relation, but there's some kind of connection—we're from the same village. He has come from our village and is staying in our house. I got him a shift job as a tub checker, but some foreman has shunted him off to loading. Won't you please help him, sir?'

'Sure, yes, definitely.' Harishankar patted Agani on the back. What was it that brought such self-confidence back into his voice? Two years ago he had lost this assurance. Today, after stepping out of the general manager's room he felt the old strength and enthusiasm surging through him again. 'These small things can be easily done, Agani, but we have to aim for something even more important. Come, let's go and sit in the eatery. I'll tell you everything.'

SIX

During the day Pradyumna had no chores. Earlier, before he started working, he would help his aunt with the cooking. Now that he had a job his aunt saw him as a possible match for Runu, and her usual standoffish attitude became tinged with some affection.

Pradyumna's demotion from tub checker to loader caused his aunt more grief than it did his uncle. She pleaded on his behalf to Uncle Agani, saying that he was not an untouchable who would take up a loading job. He was an educated Brahmin boy after all.

This had led his uncle to react angrily. 'Considerations about caste don't bear any weight in a coal mine. There are many educated boys, Brahmins included, who're doing loading work. Am I not myself a Brahmin? When I started working at the company, I had to stoop to washing the Sahibs' dirty plates, not to speak of doing loading work, which was much tougher then. I had to tie a rope to the tub cart, thread the end through a pulley, and pull it. Look at me now—I'm an electrician drawing the salary of a fifth-grade worker. Add what I earn from overtime and extra work on

Sundays to that, and I'm ready to pay income tax. Had my pride in being a Brahmin stopped me from doing my job, you wouldn't be spending money freely with both hands as you are now.'

Pradyumna had felt Uncle Agani's spite was directed at him rather than his wife. He was overwhelmed by a sense of helplessness. It seemed that no one could be bothered about what he liked, that nobody was willing to accept him as an individual with his own likes and dislikes, his personal taste in things.

Pradyumna had been helpless like this right from birth, a liability for everyone. To begin with, his birth had not been planned. By the time he was conceived, his mother, having had one son and three daughters, was exhausted. Afraid the child would be another girl, she had taken a medicine to terminate the pregnancy. Even though this did not kill the unborn Pradyumna, it was perhaps responsible for his frail health. Long after he was born he learned he was an unplanned child. When he got to know, he felt the ground beneath his feet shift. He felt completely abandoned, like someone whose entire existence was friendless and fruitless.

When he saw his uncle get angry, Pradyumna was reminded of his parents' unfulfilled wish that he would die before being born. Had he been a slave right from birth? He had no say about his birth and no say about how he lived his life; he was always at the mercy of others.

Afterwards Uncle Agani took him to the union office and pleaded with Dhruba Babu. The latter was seated in the office, surrounded by his sycophants, a large, framed photo of Hema Babu behind him on the wall. Hema Babu was the MLA for this area and a cabinet minister in the government of Odisha. Pradyumna had heard that Dhruba Babu was close to Hema Babu and that Hema Babu had stopped coming to the colliery after becoming a minister, having installed Dhruba Babu as his representative. Dhruba Babu was regarded as the living representative of the minister by many senior and superior officers.

Dhruba Babu was in an inebriated condition—his way of talking and how he looked made that clear. His addiction to alcohol was so well known that Pradyumna had heard about it when he had first arrived at the coal mine. Dhruba Babu listened to the people's grievances and difficulties for some time, after which he lambasted general manager Mr Mirchandani, project officer Mr Mishra, and sub-area manager Mr Deskmukh. Only after that did he notice Agani and ask, 'Hey you, what brings you to the union office today?'

Uncle Agani answered him respectfully. 'This nephew of mine has been newly recruited. He was working as a tub checker but was recently moved to loading.'

'Didn't your nephew know he had been hired as a loader?'

'Sir, he's a Brahmin boy; a commerce graduate. Would it be fitting for him to do loading work like an untouchable?'

'No caste considerations work in a socialist nation, you know. Here, all are equal. You bloody Agani, you spent your days licking the feet of Harishankar and you don't know this?'

Agani stomached the insults shamelessly. 'Dhruba Babu', he said, 'everything's possible for you if you try. You're talking about Harishankar. Well, you should know I cut off my ties with him when your union was formed. Our leader is Hema Babu. Who on earth's Harishankar? Whoever Hema Babu picks as the leader is our leader.'

Dhruba Babu broke into a smug smile. 'Has your nephew joined our union?'

Pradyumna did not hold the union members in a high opinion. All schemers, he thought. If anyone was exploiting the workers, it was the trade-union leaders more than the mill owners. It was as if being in trade-union politics was a quick and easy way to mint money. If you could bully people, if you were daring and could intimidate workers into giving you money, then everyone, from the police and the officers of the colliery down to the clerks, would respect you and provide you with a chair to sit on.

On payday Pradyumna had seen crowds of people in front of the payment counter, there to collect money. The grocer in the bazaar, the clothes-shop owner, the Afghan street hawker who lent money at ten per cent, and the other traders were all there. They would swoop down on the poor workers the moment they left the wages counter. The union members were also there. Five or six of them, as strong as bulls, could be spotted by their receipt books and party flags. Pradyumna had always felt these union members were as ferocious as the traders who pounced on the workers. He knew from experience that no workers volunteered to pay money—they were forced to part with it.

That day in the union office, Uncle Agani had no shame in kowtowing to Dhruba Khatua. 'He'll join up, sir. He's just started his job. It's been only three or four months.'

'What's your name?' asked Dhruba Khatua.

'Pradyumna. I go by the name of Samaru Khadia in the attendance register, though.'

'A case of impersonation then. Forget it friend. Forget it entirely. There's nothing to be done.'

While in college, Pradyumna had heard an unsavoury joke. It was in English and went like this: If a woman says 'no' then take it she means 'perhaps'. If, however, she says 'I'll try', this means she's saying 'no'. If she says 'yes', then she's no woman. Likewise, if a politician says 'yes', then he means 'I'll see'. If he says 'I'll see', then he means 'no'. If he says 'no', he's no politician.

As he left the union office Pradyumna felt crushed by humiliation and remorse. But his uncle took no notice and spoke like an eternal optimist. 'It'll be done, you'll see. To hell with that drunkard. There'll be a good outcome if money's spent.'

Pradyumna still had not repaid the two thousand rupees borrowed from his uncle to buy a card from the Employment Exchange. At the mention of more expenses he became a little frightened. His uncle probably guessed his mental state. 'Don't worry about the money', he said. 'That'll be taken care of.'

Pradyumna knew what 'taken care of' meant. Uncle Agani would be generous and Pradyumna would become so weighed down under a debt of gratitude he would not be able to say no to marrying Runu. He could not say anything. In silence they retraced their way back to the house.

The following morning Pradyumna left for the hospital after breakfast, arranged for a sick leave, and returned without picking up his medication. Now what? Where would he go? He lighted a cigarette at the paan shop. Normally, he did not smoke. After two or three puffs he coughed and threw away the cigarette. He went to a stall and got himself some tea. Then he walked up to a grocery shop and read a Hindi newspaper. The clock still had not moved past ten o'clock.

How would he pass the time? He felt suffocated at Uncle Agani's. Jhunu would be busy socializing and gossiping with her boyfriends on the veranda; his aunt would be fuming about Jhunu's behaviour. Or else Runu and Jhunu would be at each other's throat over buying bangles and ribbons or about going to the movies, smashing pots and pans. Or the mother and daughters would be picking a quarrel with a woman from the neighbourhood about someone hitting Sonu. The entire atmosphere was stifling. No one in Pradyumna's village spoke in a loud voice. Even his jobless elder brother was never reprimanded loudly by his father and mother when they became angry with him. The politeness and decorum he had seen since childhood were conspicuously absent in Uncle Agani's family. They dragged the home out into the street.

What would Pradyumna do? He went to the post office; there was no letter either from home or from Minakshi. Her last letter had arrived fifteen or twenty days ago and remained unanswered. He had not found the right time, place, or occasion to write to her. And when time, place, and occasion were present the mood was missing. Was he forgetting her? Why then did he eye the postman wistfully, hoping for a letter from her? Why did he find it so painful to write her?

Was Pradyumna changing? Was the old Pradyumna getting hidden under a layer of moss? Or maybe coal. The coating was so thick he was unable to recognize his old self beneath it. Was he changing into someone new? Into Samaru Khadia? And of course Samaru Khadia couldn't be expected to have any connection with Sarbeswar Mishra or Minakshi.

Pradyumna came out of the post office and looked back towards the colony again. The colony in Tarabahar housed two or three thousand families. Most of the houses had asbestos roofs; most of the roads were not black topped. Poverty and gloom were all around. In this vast world, how small and insignificant this colliery was! And it was in such a hellhole that he was going to spend thirty-five years of his life!

The same beaten and monotonous two-kilometre track from the colony to the pit and from the pit back to the colony day after day. Along with occasional trips to the market. There was nowhere else to go to. The sentence in the prison of Tarbahar Colliery was for a lifetime. A big world existed beyond the colliery. Pradyumna was longingly waiting for the tenderest heart in this world, who went by the name of Minakshi. He was going to forget all this.

Pradyumna heaved a sigh at the sight of the red state buses on their way to Cuttack, Bhubaneswar, or Puri. He felt like boarding one. He could be in Puri by daybreak. He suddenly remembered he had not seen the sea and the Grand Road or eaten abhada for a long time. Nor had he been able to watch the Satasankha jatra group rehearse its performances. He had not seen Minakshi for a long time. He had slept with his head in her lap only once; he had kissed her only twice. How could he give up all these promises and chose a life in exile? He had become so alienated that he was distanced not only from his familiar world, surroundings and people but also from his own name and identity.

'For the life of me I can't understand what's wrong if you pass yourself off as Samaru Khadia' was what Pradyumna knew people in the colliery would tell him. No one understood him, not Uncle Agani, not Nanda Babu, the electrician, Mitrabhanu, the peon, Ram Narayan Singh, the security guard, or Ram Avtar, the driver.

Pradyumna found himself unable to explain his feelings, despite his attempts. 'I have a name of my own. Pradyumna. My father has a name. I have an individual identity. Can I forget all this and turn into Samaru?'

'Why not?'

'Well, all these days I have lived my life as Pradyumna would have been for nothing.'

Everyone eyed him with wonder as if they had never before seen someone like Pradyumna. 'Well, what difference does it make?' asked Ram Avtar. 'My name's Chandrasekhar and I was recruited during the era of the

Company. There weren't as many rules then as now. Nor
were there all the hassles about taking up a job. The manager
sahib asked me my name and I gave it. Somehow the sahib
couldn't come to terms with the name of Chandrasekhar.
A sahib after all; a man of whims. He told me to go by the
name of Ram Avtar from then on, and I've been known by
that name ever since. Look at me. Do you see any change
in me? For the first twenty years of my life I went by the
name of Chandrasekhar; for the next twenty-five years I've
been known as Ram Avtar and will probably continue to
be known as such for another fifteen years or until I die. I
earn around two thousand rupees a month, including the
income from overtime work. I'm married. I've got my
daughter married. What loss have I suffered? If anyone calls
me by my original name, it sounds strange. I can't even
imagine that the name was ever my own.'

The other day Dhruba Babu made another comment
in the union office. 'What would have happened if you
were given the name of Dhruba Mishra or Dhruba Khatua,
instead of Samaru Khadia? Would you have felt sorry?
Maybe a little, but you'd have accepted it. But since Khadia
is an adivasi name, you react against it as a Brahmin. Isn't
that right?'

Pradyumna had kept quiet. How could he explain his
predicament? Maybe Dhruba Babu was right, maybe not. Or
it could be that Pradyumna himself did not fully understand
the reason for his own suffering. He knew only that in the
course of his metamorphosis from Pradyumna Mishra to
Samaru Khadia he had felt as if his self had been lost, as if he

had ceased to exist, as if Samaru Khadia had taken his place. The strange thing was that this Samaru Khadia was unable to forget Pradyumna Mishra, was grieving for his death. Pradyumna knew he would not be able to explain his plight to anyone.

He had heard the mining sardar, Chaturbhuja Shah, who lived in the same neighbourhood as Uncle Agani, say that his provident-fund money might be claimed by someone in the name of Samaru Khadia or Baithu Khadia. According to Shah, the most important thing to do was to change the name of Samaru Khadia back to Pradyumna's on the provident-fund register.

Shah had shown him how to do that. An affidavit had to be sworn in the subdivision court through a lawyer at a cost of ten to fifteen rupees. The affidavit should read more or less as follows: 'I, Samaru Khadia, son of Baithu Khadia, hereby change my name to Pradyumna Mishra, son of Sarbeswar Mishra, and I will be so known in all official documents.' One could then present a copy of the affidavit to the management. The union members ought to be appeased too, Shah said.

Sharma Babu, the old clerk in the provident-fund section, had cast a sharp look from under his glasses when he heard all this. Pradyumna was caught off guard. 'Did the mining sardar Chaturbhuja give you this piece of wisdom?' Sharma Babu asked. 'He's a fellow who knows how to write his name in English but can't write all the letters of the English alphabet. Since when has he started dispensing wisdom? For God's sake, don't get carried away by what he says. Once the management learns you're not Samaru Khadia, you'll get involved in an impersonation case. Do you know impersonation is forgery? It's an offence under section 420 of the Indian Penal Code. Do you realize you can be sent to jail for committing such an offence?'

'To the jail?'Agani uncle had laughed sarcastically. 'How many people can the management send to jail? How many people from Bihar, Gorakhpur, and Allahabad have passed themselves off as locals at recruitment interviews for the colliery? Isn't the management aware of this? It's fully aware. Wait, today I'll take you to Harishankar Babu.'

Harishankar Babu was Harishankar Patnaik, the former secretary of the union. Pradyumna had seen him once or twice. He did not seem to have much influence, and he was no longer in the union. Why would the management listen to him? Nor was Pradyumna favourably impressed by the union. He had not forgotten how Dhruba Babu had behaved, inebriated, that day in the union office. If Pradyumna had a say, he would have had those union fellows whipped in the street. He had no love lost for them.

But he was unable to show his uncle the hatred and regret that lay bottled up within him. He only asked, 'So what's going to be done about the recent switch from tub checker to loader?'

'That'll be taken care of; make no mistake about it', his uncle had answered. 'We'll speak to Harishankar Babu. He has a lot of experience. Even now the general manager, the deputy chief mining engineer, and the sub-area manager show him great respect. Won't they try to oblige him?'

Were his uncle's words only empty words of solace? Pradyumna could not be sure. A huge wave of helplessness swept through him. No one had a thought to spare for his own likes and dislikes, his hopes and aspirations. Everyone was so wrapped up in their own individual life that they did not have time to throw a glance at another person. Pradyumna left his uncle behind. The world was very large and it spread far and wide, but Pradyumna was all alone, alone and dangling between happiness and sorrow, hopes and aspirations, dream and success, life and death.

SEVEN

Deshmukh was at the office, but there was nothing much for him to do. He had been stripped of all power, even of the little it takes to grant leave for a day or to allow use of the office jeep for half an hour. Despite this, he was still being held to account for the production of his unit. He had absolutely no authority in the mines, where the project officer reigned supreme. The mining sardars and foremen did not like him; the managers under him did not bother to greet him. No one paid any attention to his suggestions about how to increase output, but it was he who was criticized by the project officer if there was a drop in the amount of coal.

Deshmukh rang the office bell. No sign of the peon; Deshmukh knew he wouldn't come. His stenographer, he could guess, was most likely taking dictation from someone else. If he called for him, the stenographer would probably plead he had been assigned urgent work by the deputy chief mining engineer. So he was condemned to sit in the office solely for the sake of appearance. If he left, he would have to provide an explanation to the project officer, who would make things worse by asking: 'Mr Deshmukh, if you take time off like this, how can we expect other workers to act professionally?'

Deshmukh had tried to adjust to the situation at the office, but he had failed. From somewhere deep inside a rebellious voice was rising that to be an officer was to be utterly helpless: you weren't allowed to be disobedient, or to protest.

If he had been a clerk or a labourer, he would not have had so much visibility. He would have been able to get away with disregarding the orders of his superiors, or with threatening them and lashing out at them. If he was not of a mind to work, he could have simply gone on sick leave. He could have left the office right when the bell rang at the end of office hours. As an officer, however, he was bound to obediently follow his superior's wishes. He had to prove he was 'responsible', act as if he had no personal or family life. He could not go home before his boss did. His superior might be a fool, but if this man expressed displeasure with his work no matter how well executed the work was, then he had to instantly admit his superior was right and he was wrong.

Deshmukh had long dreamed of becoming an officer. Actually, that had been his mother's dream, which he had set out to turn into reality. His mother had been widowed when he was ten years old. He was from a very conservative family, in which it was customary for widows to shave their heads. Deshmukh remembered the day very well. His father's funeral ceremony was being observed, and everyone was grief stricken. There was an enormous vacuum in Deshmukh's heart. This was his first encounter with death, and, even worse, with the death of someone close to him. That was when the trouble broke out. On his own somewhere outside, Deshmukh was trying to connect with the memory of his deceased father, trying to cope with his sense of loss. On hearing the disturbance he had come running to the courtyard. His relatives sat in a circle and his mother was standing, leaning against a pole. Her long hair fell loose below her waist. The end of her sari was tucked in at her back. Her eyes were brimming with tears. Around her sat his grandmother, uncles, the Brahmin priest, and the barber.

Grandmother, who had pressed her veil close to her tonsured head, asked: 'Tell us which one is more important: your husband, who has died, or your hair?'

Mother did not reply.

The priest: 'This is the custom, my dear child. This has to be performed for your husband's soul to find peace in heaven.'

Mother remained quiet.

The uncles: 'Bhauja, this is a matter of family honour. As a daughter-in-law in this family it's your duty to uphold its honour. What will people say if you refuse to shave your head? In these fashionable times many widows might prefer not to, but what does that have to do with us? The glorious legacy of our family, its noble tradition . . . Don't you know our ancestors held the post of minister in the royal court of Shivaji?'

Mother remained silent, her eyes tear filled. Deshmukh's paternal grandmother observed that if she was not willing to do it on her own, then it should be done by force. A stern look from my mother, however, stopped everyone in their tracks.

Although India had become independent by then, this had made little difference to the way Deshmukh was being brought up in a family where superstition was rife. His mother, who had defied such restrictions and had dared to dream her son would become an important officer, ought to have been congratulated on her courage and determination.

Instead, she was ostracized for refusing to shave off her hair. Despite having been shunned by her family, her strong desire to create a good future for her son persisted. Deshmukh was sent far away, from Maharashtra to Odisha, to work as an officer at Tarbahar Colliery. Was this a move upwards? What was so important about becoming an officer? What problem would there have been if he had not? His mother may have felt fulfilled by having made an officer out of her son, but what could Deshmukh make of himself?

His mother had taken great pains for Deshmukh to become a successful, accomplished person. After independence, when the news of Gandhi's death at the hands of a Brahmin became known, Maharashtra was gripped by anti-Brahmin riots. As a result, many Brahmins left their villages and made their way into the towns. Their land and homesteads were taken over by either Marathas or Dalits. Deshmukh's was one of many such families. His father and uncles set up a store selling cloth in a small town in Marathwada called Jalna. They lived in a joint family, a family untouched by light from the outside world. Although his grandmother never left her dark corner nor saw the light of day, she was the head of the family. Her obedient sons did not dream of contradicting her orders.

Deshmukh's mother was like a lamp in that dark house. She raged against the extinction of the light, something that was attempted there a thousand times. It was difficult to say how effective that small flame from a clay lamp was in dispelling the darkness of a feudal and conservative mindset, for the brutal truth was that the gloom of the eighteenth and nineteenth centuries had shut out the light of the twentieth.

His mother received none of the income from the cloth store. The only way she could assert a right to the ancestral house was by crawling into a six by ten foot room, hardly more than a hole, for shelter. Despite being a daughter-in-law in a Brahmin family, she was forced out onto the street to work as a maid in other people's homes. Deshmukh's grandmother and uncles felt she had brought shame to the family. From his early childhood he had understood the basic facts about survival. He had felt the cruel tug of hunger in his belly, seen tears in his mother's eyes, witnessed the reprimands from his grandmother and the insulting words from his uncles, and heard his mother's heart-rending sighs in the dead of night. All this had increased his love for his mother more and more.

Deshmukh looked around him. His office was divided by a wooden partition and was almost bare, with only a

Godrej table and chair, a telephone, and a rack for files. The air cooler was the only item adding a touch of luxury. The project officer's chamber was much more tastefully furnished, with an Iranian carpet, a conference table, a fine wall-mounted bookshelf, graphs, and a board listing previous incumbents. The air cooler was fitted into a hole in the wall, and the lavatory attached to the office was luxurious. The stenographer sat in an adjoining room. The office was always under watch, and the peon on the alert for the sound of the call bell. When measured against the official grandeur of the project officer's room, the starkness of his own made Deshmukh feel miserable. The weight of this terrible feeling of inferiority was almost too much for him. He felt as if he was a wild shrub from the jungle planted by mistake in a beautifully decorated park. It was as if his very presence and existence was shameful for Tarbahar Colliery.

Deshmukh came out of his office. His jeep was not at its usual place, standing under the portico outside his office. Mr Mishra might arrive at any moment, as a result of the enquiries Deshmukh had been making about where the jeep had gone. 'If you had something you wanted to say', he would remark, 'you could have said it to me. Why are you hell bent on maligning me in front of these useless people? You ought to learn to be a responsible officer, Mr Deshmukh. Your habits and style of functioning are resembling those of a clerk or a loader.'

Deshmukh knew he could not protest. He was a senior officer; he had to set standards for obedience and discipline.

Had his mother's life been so hard, had she had to put up with so much ill treatment for him to become an officer, only so that he would have to keep up appearances, put up with the hostility of one and all, like some slave? Would his mother ever learn about his utter misery?

His family had no way of realizing any of this because none of them had ever been in service. In fact, no one in his family had risen above the rank of a schoolmaster. Before getting employed Deshmukh had not seen the city of Mumbai. Nor had he been to Pune. The scenic natural beauty of Lonavala was unknown to him. Before studying in college he had not even been to Aurangabad, the city nearest to where he lived. It was in college that he discovered the bigger and wider world. During his two-year stay as a student in Aurangabad he did not visit the caves of Ajanta and Ellora; or Bibi Ka Maqbara, the mini Taj Mahal; or the tomb of Aurangzeb. He leaned more towards politics. At first, he joined the Shiv Sena. The booklets he read about the unification of Maharashtra and the future of the Hindu religion drew him towards the ideology of the Rashtriya Swayamsevak Sangh (RSS). He went out on processions taken out by the Sangh every morning; he also went to the akhara and learned how to wield a lathi. It was when he was a committed follower of the RSS that a lecture by Dattatreya Joshi catapulted him towards the emerging ideology of the Dalit Panther Movement.

It was Professor Joshi who explained how politics in Maharashtra were now under the control of the Marathas and how, by using the anti-Brahmin agitation of 1947, they had broken the back of the Brahmin community. From Professor Joshi he learned there were two main currents—Maratha and Dalit—in the political culture of Maharashtra. Brahmins had to choose between them. What would they gain by siding with the Marathas? Surely the Marathas would not leave any place for them. It was far better for them to side with the Dalits. The historical underdevelopment of the Dalit community would ensure it would remain subservient to the Brahmins. If the anti-high-caste sentiments of the Dalits could be turned against the Marathas, it would be the Brahmins who would stand to gain.

*

The only mark of his status as an officer was his jeep, but it was not always at his disposal. There were times when the driver did not show up, and others when the jeep was sent to run errands. Deshmukh asked a clerk where his jeep was, though he realized the clerk would not know.

When the clerk answered he didn't in fact know, Deshmukh flew into a rage. 'What on earth do you know? Only how to avoid work and do nothing? Go back inside and get to work.'

The clerk was flustered. He was probably taking time off for some tea or a paan or to have a smoke. Deshmukh's harsh reprimand stunned him into silence. He panicked and made a hasty retreat.

Deshmukh came back to his room. He wondered why he had given the clerk such a tongue-lashing for no good reason.

He remembered the remark someone had once made to him: 'We Indians are always barking in the wrong place.'

Deshmukh phoned the motor-vehicle division and found out that his office jeep was being used to ferry managers to and from the pit. When he became angry and demanded an explanation, the person in charge answered, 'No other jeep was available, Sir. Mishra Sahib said . . . '

Mishra Sahib! Mentioning his name was like invoking an all-powerful, invincible weapon. Confronted with it Deshmukh dissolved like a coward, like a reptile, like a piece of melting ice, and was annihilated. He could not go on. If he said anything more, the tale of his reaction would reach Mr Mishra, who would call him the following day and give him an earful.

*

The brilliant lecture by Professor Joshi drove home the point that politics is entirely a game of opportunism. Deshmukh's curiosity was aroused by this, and he joined the Dalit Panthers and engrossed himself in serious discussions on issues such as the need for Dalits to convert to Buddhism, Maratha communalism and the new form it had taken under the Shiv Sena, communism, the new Buddhism, etc.

Only after he became associated with the Dalit movement did he learn about Marxism and was introduced to terms like 'exploitation', 'the proletariat', and 'the bourgeoisie'. Before subscribing to Marxist doctrine he had become disillusioned with the caste-based politics of the Dalits. When he went to Nagpur to study engineering he formed some sort of vague impression of communism without reading any of the writings of Marx, Engels, or Lenin and became a member of the student federation. Later, he did attempt to gain a purely superficial understanding of Marxism by speaking and reading about it. But when it occurred to him he could manage perfectly well without doing that, his reading stopped. He realized he had not seen anyone turn into a communist as a result of trying to decipher *Das Kapital*. Besides, his idea of who were members of the proletariat was modelled on his mother, the epitome for him of the oppressed, having been able to bring him up only through her hard physical labour. His mother's rebellion against conservative family values had led him towards Marxism; this was why he left the RSS and became a communist.

After completing his engineering degree in mining, Deshmukh was hired as a trainee junior engineer by Coal India and was posted in the coal mines in West Bengal run by Eastern Coalfields. The unquestioned sway of the communist-run trade unions and their activities there soon led him to become disillusioned with communism. By now he knew that politics was a game played for personal advantage, simply a cover for placing one's own interests above those of community and caste, and that ideals, theory, and hypotheses were used to mask blatant self-interest. In the eyes of Deshmukh, all political leaders were alike, whether from the RSS, the CPI/CPIM, Janata, or Congress.

*

Mr Mishra's manner seemed to indicate that he considered Deshmukh to be inexperienced in diplomacy, that he wouldn't be able to take on the leaders of the trade union. He was always advising Deshmukh to stay away from the unions and eyed him suspiciously if he found him talking to a union member. Deshmukh knew that if he was spotted Mr Mishra would launch a full investigation, with various sources providing a detailed report on what had transpired between him and the person to whom he was speaking. Mr Mishra had spies posted everywhere, and Deshmukh's activities and movements were under surveillance.

Mr Mishra would also warn Deshmukh from time to time: 'Please don't give these union folks any kind of opportunity or encouragement Mr Deshmukh. You may not be aware of this, but these people are able to launch a battle of the scale of the Mahabharat on the basis of something trivial. Any conciliatory or confrontational stand on your part could disrupt the peace in the unit. If you're faced with any policy decision or union matter, please refer them to me at once.'

Mr Mishra had very good relations with people in the union. Deshmukh simply could not stand its secretary, that drunkard Dhruba Khatua, with whom Mr Mishra was chummy. Dhruba Khatua had no respect for Deshmukh. Often Deshmukh wondered how Mr Mishra could cultivate a drunk, shameless self-promoter like Khatua. Only someone who was morally and culturally degenerate could tolerate people like him. Deshmukh would never have been able to do that.

The general manager, Mr Mirchandani, once asked Deshmukh, 'Do you engage in politics Mr Deshmukh? Every lower-ranking executive in India does. I'm not talking about party politics, but the politics of survival, the politics to save your job.'

Mr Mirchandani did not have a favourable impression of Mr Mishra, but the differences between them were not noticeable from the outside. Once Mirchandani Sahib had told Deshmukh, 'Why do you accept Mr Mishra's one-upmanship with such good grace? You have your own power and jurisdiction. Why do you allow Mr Mishra to meddle in your affairs? You know you're supposed to take decisions on things that come under your jurisdiction. So why should you accept Mr Mishra's intervention? You should reach out to the union people. It will be even better for you if you have good relations with them. Get them to turn against Mr Mishra, and then you'll see how Mr Mishra will come scurrying to your doorstep.'

Could his mother have imagined the depths to which an officer in a nationalized organization in independent India had to stoop? Could she have known how frightened, apprehensive, and lonely this person would be beneath his officer's trappings? How futile indeed were the dreams his mother had had for him for so long!

Deshmukh yearned for his mother. Despite his repeated insistence, she had never visited him where he was working. Did she feel ill at ease about accepting Anita's independent spirit? Deshmukh thought that was the case. His mother loved him dearly. She had put her son above everything else in the world; she had spent every breath on making him a success. The prospect of this same son being shared with another person, being loved by another woman, the very idea this son might love this other person back—his mother could not bear this harsh truth. This was why his mother's anger was directed towards Anita and why she had distanced herself from Deshmukh after his marriage. She had embraced her confinement in that narrow and dingy cell measuring six feet by ten.

Deshmukh had not visited his mother in a long time. Earlier he used to send her money, but even he did not remember when the remittances had come to a stop. His mother had never asked for it either. She had withdrawn all claims on Deshmukh without a murmur of protest. Did this mean her heart was broken? Deshmukh should have run to her, setting aside all hesitation. When he was a child, he had never been bothered by his mother's anger, irritation, or scolding. It was on her lap he had always sought refuge. Yet these days it seemed to Deshmukh as if he hardly ever missed the comfort of her lap. He grew sad thinking about this. What could his mother be doing now, at this very moment?

*

Deshmukh stepped out of his office. The clerks, watchmen, peons, and workers walking on the office veranda ignored him. He couldn't help but notice the project officer's jeep parked out in front, and, of course, the peon, as he quickly entered Mr Mishra's office and exited it equally swiftly. The watchman was ever alert as he stood at attention. Deshmukh went out through the gate. He knew his leaving the office would be reported to Mr Mishra immediately. Mr Mishra's spies were watching him all the time. He found himself sinking into depression the moment he thought about this. He wanted to leave his job and go back to Jalna. He wanted to make a fresh start. Above all else, he wanted to find his way back onto his mother's lap.

Deshmukh returned home. He opened the gate and stood on the veranda. Anita had spent a lot of effort making the house trim and tidy. The garden was full of flowering trees, and potted plants dotted the entire veranda, one corner of which was covered with money plants and cactus. In the centre was a table surrounded by cane chairs, and in a tub suspended from the roof was a table rose. Anita was a woman of cultivated tastes. He had not yet fully understood her. She was an independent thinker, but vanity lurked somewhere within her, probably due to Deshmukh's important position. Of course, she had never been brusque with his mother. Never had a rude remark escaped her lips, nor any complaints or words of censure. But yet there was a certain coldness between the two.

Anita opened the door and exclaimed, 'It's you!'

She was dressed up. Was she headed out? Did she have an engagement? This was not his usual hour to return home. She was a free-spirit, and she did not want to be under Deshmukh's control. To be fair, he had never been tempted to assert his authority over her. A principal reason for his tension with Mr Mishra was Anita: she had an uncontrollable urge to stand up to his wife. Of course, Deshmukh had never tried to pressurize Anita into being loyal to Mrs Mishra.

'I'm meeting with the wife of the general manager', Anita said. 'We've made a decision to initiate special activities through the Rotary Club. An adult education drive in the labourers' colony will be the first. This is to be finalized at today's meeting.'

Deshmukh leaned back on the sofa. How dearly was he paying for this house, with its display of wealth and status, for Anita's stylish lifestyle. What an irony! Deshmukh was at his lowest after fulfilling his mother's dream and her painstaking efforts to make him successful, while Anita was happy and contented as an officer's wife! Deshmukh remembered the cave-like six by ten room in the house in Jalna. His mother's image flashed through his mind. She was wearing a blue handloom sari traditionally, with one end passing between her legs and tucked at the back. He spoke almost inaudibly. 'I'm giving up my job, Anita. I'm returning to Jalna.'

Anita slumped down on the sofa. She ran her fingers through Deshmukh's hair and asked, 'What's the matter? Have you had a stressful day at work?'

She drew him to her chest. The fragrance of a foreign perfume emanated from her body. Deshmukh once again saw the scene of his father's last rites. His mother was surrounded by his grandmother, uncles, the priest, and the barber. Anita planted a kiss on Deshmukh's forehead.

Another scene arose before him. His mother stood, leaning against a pole, her eyes awash with tears. Deshmukh held Anita in a tight embrace.

'My make-up, dear, please mind my make-up and don't crumple my sari.'

Deshmukh called out in a feeble voice: 'Mother! Mother!'

Swimming through the mist, Deshmukh was journeying towards the past. As a boy he had slept through the night on a mat in the smallest room of that small house in Jalna, the back of his head singed by his mother's long sighs. Night after night had passed that way. The sudden ringing of the bell startled Anita. As she moved towards the mirror to tidy her dress, she called out to the servant boy to go and see who was at the door. Deshmukh followed Anita to the mirror. A mischievous smile lurked in her eyes. For a long time now there had been nothing intimate between them. Was it appropriate for them to fan the dying embers back to life? Deshmukh was morose. He was thinking of giving up his job. The thought of his mother was troubling him. For Anita he felt neither love nor intimacy. And yet?

The servant boy came in. 'Harishankar Patnaik is at the door', he announced.

'Who's this Harishankar Patnaik?' Anita asked in disbelief. 'I don't think anyone by that name has ever come to see you.'

'He's a retired trade-union member. He works as a clerk in the general manager's office.' Having said this, Deshmukh told the servant, 'Ask him to sit in the drawing room. Get him a cup of tea.'

Deshmukh looked at his reflection in the mirror. He looked older than his forty years. Anita, by contrast, seemed fresh and young. She was hastily rearranging her make-up; she was already very late.

EIGHT

Harishankar slept badly. The meeting to announce the new union was to take place at daybreak. At first, permission for the meeting had been denied by the colliery's project officer, Mr Mishra, on the grounds that forming a second union was out of the question while a recognized union was already in place. But Harishankar managed to obtain permission from the general manager, Mr Mirchandani.

Many celebrated the overcoming of this obstacle as Harishankar's first victory. Of course, he did not let anyone know that Mr Mirchandani was sympathetic to the new union and tacitly supporting it. Certain things needed to be hidden from the workers, among them the covert support of the management.

This was not Harishankar's first meeting; as general secretary of Hema Babu's union he had organized many. But this was going to be the first of his own union, and he was on edge. The microphone and speakers in the union office were under Dhruba Khatua's control. Harishankar had arranged to rent a set. There had been some difficulty getting their hands on an album of patriotic songs. Such songs were badly needed to attract workers arriving for the morning shift or those returning home, tired out, from the previous night of work. But patriotic songs were hard to find in the market these days; film songs had taken their place. Agani Hota was in favour of the latter, arguing that when it came to pulling in a crowd there was nothing better. But Harishankar was not convinced. He searched the club and found a record of patriotic songs from the cinema. The bhajan dear to Mahatma Gandhi, 'Ram Dhun', was nowhere to be found. It was no longer in demand in the market.

However, Harishankar still felt something was missing. He knew there was a record of 'Your name is Allah, Your name is Ishwar' in the office of the old union. The Dhruba gang had stopped playing it; only cheap film songs blared at their meetings. This was not how things had been when Harishankar was in charge. The closest he had come to making a concession to the cinema was to play the hugely popular patriotic song by Lata Mangeshkar, 'Oh, people of my country'. For him, no meeting was complete without 'Ram Dhun' being played.

All the preparations for the meeting had been made. The agenda was ready. Permission from the police station had been obtained. There had been enough publicity; word had spread throughout Tarbahar Colliery about the birth of a new union. Harishankar realized that he had once again become the focus of people's attention, after a long time. Once again, people were looking at him with interest; either greeting him out of fear or respect, or avoiding him. His presence was once again beginning to be felt in the colliery.

Harishankar tossed and turned throughout the night. He dreamed about the meeting as he slept fitfully and left the house at the crack of dawn. The boys working at the nearby tea stall were not yet up. The coal oven had not been lit and the owner of the tea shop had not yet arrived. Harishankar desperately needed a cup of tea. He was unlikely to get it at his own house. But who else would make him a cup of tea so early in the morning? He went to Agani Hota's quarters and called for him to come out.

A bleary-eyed Agani Hota, clad in a lungi and undershirt, a towel covering his head, left the house wearing slippers. He sat down in the tea shop. 'Patnaik Babu', he told Harishankar. 'Your speech should be stirring. People have to be fired up. Your speech should be more electrifying than Khatua's.'

Harishankar told Agani Hota what he was going to say. He would stress the role a trade union had to play in a nationalized organization. He would speak about how the project officer's underhanded attempt to stall today's meeting had exposed the conspiracy by the bureaucrats in a public-sector undertaking.

'What will be gained by targeting only the project officer?' asked Agani Hota. 'Our union's out-and-out anti-management stance should be highlighted. Keep some choice words ready for Deshmukh and the general manager.' Harishankar did not react to Agani's words. He was thinking about his visit to Deshmukh's house the day before. Seeing him up close Harishankar realized Deshmukh was not as simple and ingenuous as he might seem. But then he could be of advantage to Harishankar. The man seemed quite subdued, overshadowed by the project officer. He had started by talking down to Harishankar, offering to give his career a lift up. Harishankar had to subtly remind him that he had come on the advice of the general manager to give Deshmukh a lift up, not to get one from him.

Upon returning home from the tea stall Agani introduced Harishankar to his nephew. 'He's my nephew; we're from the same village. I have got him on the payroll of the colliery as a casual loader, but under the name of Samaru Khadia.'

A case of impersonation! Hoping to scare Agani, he asked him, 'Agani, do you know what an 'impersonation case' is? Why have you run a risk by getting your nephew appointed in such a way?'

'Sir, you are well aware of the job situation', Agani answered in a worried tone. 'My nephew has come from far away. What can be gained by informing Hema Babu about it? Is it possible to get a job in the colliery these days, especially without a diploma or certificate? The other day you yourself saw the row over the interview for a clerk's position, and the interview has not even taken place yet. And then there's the matter of money, sir. These days it's money, not self-respect, prestige, and honour, that's in demand. Tell me, who looks favourably upon someone landing a lectureship at a private college after an MA degree, earning five to six hundred rupees per month? A labourer's job for two to two-and-a-half thousand rupees a month is considered more respectable.'

'I'm not talking about money, Agani. Impersonation is deception, a kind of swindling. He could lose his job at any time. Besides, someone who does that can always be blackmailed.'

'Who cares about such things at the colliery? Didn't the great Mr. Mahtab, our ex-chief minister, once say that if you made the 'unfair' 'fair' the problem would be solved? Everybody here knows it's normal to get a job through impersonation.'

Pradyumna cut in. 'What will become of me, sir? What about my job? My future? My own name?' he asked.

Harishankar eyed the young man with interest. How old could he be? Maybe twenty-one or twenty-two. His son's age. How to tell him that getting a job by fraud is like cheating oneself? What would happen to this young man? Would he work in this colliery all his life under an assumed name? Would he live out the rest of his life by proxy? Would he have to give up his retirement benefits without any claim? Would his children be able to file for his pension?

'Look, no one can be sure what will happen, and it's difficult to straighten out a twisted case like yours', said Harishankar. 'If the management agrees, then you may be able to change your name through an affidavit. But then everything depends on whether the people in charge support you, whether they'll risk doing that. You'd better wait. Let our union come into existence, and then we'll see what can be done.'

Agani and Harishankar made their way to the pithead with Pradyumna trailing behind. There was no one there.

The miners in the pit had not yet come out. The coal oven in the canteen was lit and smoke was billowing out. The timekeepers were sitting around comfortably or sleeping, their feet up on the table. Seeing Harishankar, one of them called out, 'Hello Netaji! Don't you have a meeting today?'

*

Agani walked ahead and stood near the opening to the pit on the slope. The pithead was filled with old and discarded tubs, iron rods, and items of all kinds. Harishankar had come to the colliery thirty-five years earlier. There had been no pithead here then; the whole area had been covered with trees. Only one pit, number fourteen, was in operation at the time. Deserted now, no one looked in its direction anymore, even by mistake. It was covered in wild shrubs, and was probably full of snakes.

He remembered himself standing at the pithead, as an eighteen- or nineteen-year-old young man, his fear-filled eyes scanning the new scene in front of him. The people, the objects, the houses—everything had seemed strange. It was as though he had planted his feet in a new world.

Someone had then called out for Harishankar. He turned around and saw a white sahib in shorts and a helmet standing before him. The country had already become independent, and the white sahibs had left for their own country. This white man seemed to be an anomaly in this country of brown bodies. He discovered later this man was

Ferguson sahib, the manager of the colliery, its highest-ranking officer.

Ferguson sahib, despite being such a mighty officer and belonging to the clan of sahibs, was entirely without pride or condescension. He used to go down into the mines with the workers from various sections and work for eight hours flat. Unlike now, women were not forbidden to enter the mines. Ferguson had married one of them. A year or two after Harsihankar began working there Ferguson had fought with the Company and returned to his own country, leaving his wife and two fair-skinned sons behind. One of his sons had set up a betel shop in the market. The other took to gambling. Harishankar often saw him roaming through the town in a hopeless state with a notebook and pencil in hand.

Thanks to Ferguson sahib Harishankar did not have to run around looking for a job. He had called Harishankar over and asked, 'Do you want a job? Do you want to work in the coal mines?'

Harishankar had never dreamt of finding a job so quickly. He had three younger brothers; his house in the village was dilapidated and unthatched; his widowed mother was unable to afford even a plain white sari. And hunger, hunger without respite. Fire burned in four bellies all the time. Aboard the bus after he left home, Harishankar had been filled with remorse. How would he land a job? Couldn't one just end up with a bundle of cash? It was inevitable he would return home empty handed. The twenty rupees his mother had arranged for by pawning her earrings was going to go waste.

But then, 'Would you care for a job?' Ferguson sahib had asked. 'Do you have any academic qualifications?'

'I attended school up to first class but could not continue my studies because there wasn't enough money. But I know English very well, sir.'

In those days the eleventh standard of the matriculation was referred to as the first class, an expression denoting prestige and sophistication.

'Oh, that will do just fine. You're overqualified in fact. You need a white-collar job. Well, you'll be an attendance clerk. You'll write down the names and whereabouts of everyone who goes into the pit. You'll show me the list every evening.'

It was a splendid job! Harishankar had been ready to work as a labourer. In the meantime, he had spent all but one of the twenty rupees his mother had given him. That was not enough for a ticket to go back home.

'Your per diem wage will be twelve annas. In addition, the company will give you thirty seers of paddy and four litres of kerosene every month.'

Twelve annas a day, thirty seers of paddy, and four litres of kerosene every month! How much did that all add up to? Without realizing it, Harishankar's face had broken into a smile. Presently his pay was two-and-a-half thousand a month, but for someone who had not even been able to attend the first class of matriculation the wages offered to him then had seemed as valuable as gold.

*

Harishankar returned to the present when he heard a song
being played over the speaker Om Prakash had installed
in a tree. A devotional song to Lord Jagannath rang out
first. Once again Harishankar remembered the missing
recording of 'Ram Dhun'. The old order was breaking
up, vanishing. How quickly things changed! Standing
at the pithead of Tarbahar Colliery one could not even
imagine pit number fourteen had ever existed. Yet it all
seemed to have happened only yesterday. Yes, yesterday!
Likewise, in a day or two Harishankar himself would
not be around anymore. Nor would this pit remain. But
humans would and so would the world. The day would
still dawn and the sun would rise. There would be fresh
dew on the blades of grass. But no Harishankar to witness
the rejuvenated world. The very thought of this made
him restless and morose.

Today was the day his union would be born. Was this
any time to be so cynical? Hope has always been the pillar
supporting everything, including unions and politics. There
was no room for despair. Harishankar tore himself away
from such gloomy thoughts.

Om Prakash had begun the preliminaries of the
meeting, alternating between his mother tongue, Hindi,
and broken Odia. 'Friends, a meeting has been called by
the Tarbahar Colliery workers' union at the Tarbahar
pithead at 8 a.m. today. Esteemed leader Sri Harishankar
Patnaik will grace the meeting as the chief speaker. You
are requested to ensure the meeting is successful by
attending in large numbers.'

Agani Hota approached Harishankar. 'What do you think of the arrangements for the meeting, Netaji?' he asked. 'Will there be a big crowd?'

For Harishankar, it was not important whether a large or small crowd turned up. Earlier, of course, he had cared about 'the people' and 'the masses'. What would people think? Would he lose face before them? Would people come forward to support him? But after becoming a minister, Hema Babu had laughed off these apprehensions. 'The masses! The people! They belong to no one', he had said. 'They won't remember you in the least no matter what you do for them. Very ungrateful, these masses of yours. Indian voters never vote for a candidate; they vote for a party, a symbol, or candidates nominated by their favourite leader for their supposedly patriotic virtues. Even Rama, Dama, or Shyama would win if put forward to contest the election. Do voters really have any personal knowledge of the candidates for Lok Sabha? Have they seen them with their own eyes? Many members of Parliament win without campaigning in all parts of their constituencies. Secondly, the so-called masses are also very disloyal. No matter how much you work for them, if their personal interests aren't served, they'll turn against you. So, the best way to keep the masses bound to you is to manufacture needs and then meet them, create trouble and then fix their problems and pose as their saviour.'

At first, Harishankar had been unable to accept this. Despite witnessing the decadence and erosion of values, his idealism had not been extinguished and he did not want to accept such cynicism. But later, when he thought about it, especially after leaving the union, he realized Hema Babu's words had not been entirely untrue, they were in fact what are called 'bitter truths'.

By 7.45 the crowd at the meeting site had begun to swell. Agani, Pradyumna, and Om Prakash were trying to persuade the miners emerging from the pit to sit down. Agani came to Harishankar and asked, 'Should we take these people out on a march? Maybe get them to shout slogans against the project officer right in front of his chambers?'

'No, don't bother', answered Harishankar. 'The miners from the first shift won't be here as they're at work. Those who have just finished the night shift must be exhausted. Let's not strain them any further.'

At this point Harishankar caught a glimpse of Dhruba Khatua's motorcycle. His feet began to tremble. He could see Dhruba calling over someone and questioning him—probably about the meeting. Harishankar felt ill at ease. This meeting was not against Dhruba Khatua; it was in fact his first declaration of war against Hema Babu. So far, he had been singing Hema Babu's praise. Why was he changing his tune today? How would he show Hema Babu in a negative light?

Seeing Dhruba Khatua, Agani raced forward, grabbed the microphone and shouted, 'Death to Dhruba Khatua! Death to Dhruba Khatua!'

A cry rose from the assembled crowd: 'Death to Dhruba Khatua!'

'Death to the company's agent!'

The agitated voice rose again: 'Death to the company's agent!'

'Exploitation and mafia rule will not work.'

'Will not work, will not work.'

'Death to Hema Babu.'

'Death to him, death to him.'

The thunderous slogans arising from this charged up sea of humanity warmed Harishankar's heart. So he did have the support of the people! All these people who had assembled here—if he got their consent, he could upend the earth. Who said 'the masses' meant nothing? Harishankar felt the masses were the personification of power. Otherwise, these slogans would not have given him back his lost confidence.

Dhruba Khatua was hurriedly walking towards the manager's office. Om Prakash came over to Harishankar. 'Agani Babu is calling for you', he said. 'Come and start the meeting.'

Before Harishankar's speech Agani gave a short introduction. 'Comrades! I'm here to tell you about the enormous conspiracy that is victimizing all the workers. What's more, I'm going to tell you how Hema Babu and the management are working together to exploit workers. How Hema Babu thought all thorns had been cleared by having your beloved leader, Harishankar Babu, the one who always raised his voice against exploitation, thrown out of the union. But Harishankar Patnaik won't die. Harishankar Patnaik is not just a name; he's a voice, a conscience, another name for the class of workers. If Harishankar was killed today, tomorrow hundreds of Harishankar Patnaiks would arise. The voice of resistance will come wafting over from all directions. We are all bound to unite against the forces of oppression, misrule, and corruption; in this fight we have nothing to lose but our chains. There's a whole world for us to gain.'

The meeting site resounded with applause. The under manager, the foreman, the timekeepers, staff from the lamp cabin, and some workers stood on the veranda of the pit office. But Dhruba Khatua was nowhere to be seen. Harishankar could not spot his motorcycle anywhere. When had the man made his escape? He must have given instructions to his followers to note down the speech.

Agani Hota continued his flight of oratory. 'We have to come together, brothers. We put our lives on the line, but the managers enjoy the fruits of our labour. It is they who get promoted. What do workers get? Only a few rupees. What else? We have to know who are with us and who are against us, who will stand by our side in our times of grief, and who will exploit us using chicanery and threats. From today, we must prepare for battle.'

Thunderous applause once again. Agani was adept at making speeches; even Hema Babu had often praised his skill. But Harishankar had observed that they were devoid of content: Agani's speech excited the workers and made them break into frenzied clapping, but they lacked substance. Most speeches were like that these days: nothing ever really got said; they were all empty, explosive rhetoric that had been memorized. Everyone spoke in the same formulaic manner.

Harishankar could not make up his mind about what he would say when his turn came. Unlike Agani, he was not good at giving electrifying speeches. Hema Babu had once told him: 'You haven't been able to master the art of giving speeches, Harishankar. How will you become a leader, a neta, if you don't know how to speak? Can someone become a singer without knowing how to play a harmonium? How can someone become a political leader without being able to make a speech, especially the kind of speech that will drive the audience wild with clapping?'

Harishankar began. 'Friends, as you all know, we have all gathered here today because we have decided to form a new union. A question may arise: why do we need a new union when one already exists? This is a difficult question. Each one of us should ask himself this question. Friends, simply creating a new union is not our goal. Our goal . . . '

'Our goal?' Harishankar paused for a short time. 'Our goal? What is the goal behind forming a new union?' Smiling a little, he continued. 'Our goal is to assert our presence, our existence. It was in the nineteenth century that workers became imbued with a new consciousness. They realized that they were losing the right to the products of their own labour, that a third party was profiting from what they produced. This third party had absolutely no role in production. Friends, the avowed aim of the union is to prevent employers from exploiting workers. Well, many will raise a question here—private companies, driven by profits, cease to exist if an organization has been nationalized. If so, who is the employer? Well, in such a case, the government is the employer. Is it fair to put the government of a country that has adopted socialism on par with capitalists? It is true that nationalized organizations cannot be put into the category of capitalists. But the bureaucrats who run these organizations are, through their actions and ways of thinking, no different from the capitalists of the nineteenth century. They are oblivious to the goals of public-sector organizations. They put a higher value on increasing productivity than thinking about the welfare of the workers, and the increase in productivity is not even determined by the government or the nation. It is the bureaucrats who want to raise the bar and exceed their own targets. The poor workers have to bear the brunt of all this. They resort to techniques that don't respect safety norms; no trick or stratagem is beneath them to extract more work and pay less. They don't balk at breaking the law if that leads to higher productivity.'

Agani got up from his seat and whispered into Harishankar's ear. 'Netaji, your speech should be fiery. The crowd won't warm up to you if you speak in such abstractions. You have to use expletives against the project officer, the general manager, and the others.'

Harishankar looked around and noticed that people had started to leave the meeting. He cleared his throat and resumed. 'All of you must know that the union we had before, the one that dated back to the era of the private company, was militant in character. At that time we provided fitting responses to the injustice and vindictive acts of the Company. The union that exists now is a handmaiden of the management. What can this union, created by the management, do other than look after the interests of management?'

Harishankar could see his speech had still not been able to rouse the crowd. No one was clapping. Some had started to leave when he was right in the middle of it; very few were left by the time he finished. The crowd was so thin his spirits were dashed. With great difficulty, he quickly wound up, not forgetting to announce that a new union was being formed with Agani Hota as the president. Agani Hota stood up and declared that as the president of the new union he was proposing the name of Harishankar as the general secretary. It was up to the people present to second this proposal.

Only thirty to forty members remained in the audience, half of whom, Harishankar realized, were themselves hoping to become members of the executive body of the new union. Harishankar was elected the general secretary with the aid of those who put up their hand for him.

Agani formally read out the names of the members of the acting executive body and announced that the election of the office bearers of the new union would be held in two to three months, after a list of members had been compiled. After the meeting was over Agani spoke to Harishankar, barely concealing his irritation. 'Netaji, you simply ruined the meeting with your speech. Does anyone give speeches like that?'

Harishankar gave an embarrassed smile.

The reaction to the meeting was not long in coming. In the evening, he received the news that members of Dhruba Khatua's gang had started a brawl; Om Prakash had ended up with a broken arm.

NINE

Pradyumna had never been on an airplane, nor seen the inside of a five-star hotel. He had never visited Nepal or Bangladesh, let alone Paris or New York. He had never caught a glimpse of the Himalayas. Darjeeling, Kashmir, Kanyakumari, Goa—all these places had been beyond his reach. And not only these, Pradyumna had not even been to many of the regions in his home state of Odisha, such as Mayurbhanj, Koraput, Keonjhar, Phulbani, or Kalahandi.

He remembered playing with a globe when he was little, trying to identify the longitudes and latitudes, the oceans, and the borderlines separating countries and continents on the colourful sphere. Intrigued, he took delight in tracing the air routes marked in red between countries and continents, routes linking Kolkata, Delhi, Mumbai, Karachi, Cairo, Moscow, Paris, London, Washington, Tokyo, etc.

His father had once told him that if he didn't study hard he would not be able to travel to foreign lands. Pradyumna could not say he had dedicated himself to his studies. He had received the first division in his matriculation exams, but in the Intermediate Science Examination, with Physics,

Chemistry, and Biology as the subjects, he had only managed to get a second division. He was unable to make it through the medical entrance test. Then he switched over to commerce for his bachelor's degree. Right up to the very day of the examination he had been unable to understand anything he was taught. The core subjects of commerce as mentioned above—such as money and banking, and public finance—were beyond him. When the results came out, Pradyumna found to his dismay he had not passed. He did not think it was worthwhile to sit for the supplementary examination, but, yielding to his father's demand, he did. With no preparation, and without an opportunity or a desire to study, of course he did not get through. Then he sat for the finals and failed. And after that for the supplementary, and failed once again. He gave up on examinations. Everyone in his family assumed he would never pass.

He was unable to make up his mind about what to do with his life; he had never set any goals for himself. Everyone in the family had gone to school, and so he had too. After finishing school he had continued on to college. He had written poetry for some time, but had not sent his poems to any of the magazines. He had kept them near to his heart, as if they were his closely-guarded secrets—a source both of *punya*—merit—and of *papa*—sin. Each poem overflowed with grief over failing to make Minakshi his own. But he soon lost his taste for poetry. For a while he staged some plays, but then he lost the election and could not become the drama secretary. He had no special inclination for politics, but had once fallen foul of his pro-Congress father when he wore the symbol of the Janata Party and launched an attack on the Congress for declaring the Emergency. His father's reprimand—that Pradyumna's future was bleak—was quoted by his younger sister even now, to rub in the insult. 'Father predicted it', she would say. 'You'll amount to nothing. Your future's bleak.'

Neither a poet nor a politician, Pradyumna didn't even make a name for himself by putting on plays. Although he engaged in discussions with his friends about how to successfully crack competitive examinations, he never thought of actually taking them. Nor did he start preparing for them, as students usually did, before graduating. He had no idea how he would answer the usual question: what do you want to do Pradyumna? Didn't he dream of at least becoming an ordinary clerk? Did he want to be an officer? Or a businessman? Or an industrialist? Did he dream of operating a trawler out of the port of Paradeep? Of owning a cinema hall or an eatery? Did he think he would become the owner of a press and publish a monthly magazine? Were these his dreams? No, since he did not have any. Once transformed into Samaru Khadia in this colliery he came to realize he had never wanted such an existence. The life of a Samaru Khadia was beyond his imagination.

Pradyumna was lost in thought, sitting and sipping tea. He had drifted far away from Om Prakash, who was sitting next to him and chatting away about the pithead meeting that morning. He got lost in a jungle of stray and random memories: the Grand Road in Puri, the sea beach, rehearsals for the village jatra party, weed-infested pond banks, coconut

trees, curd and flattened rice blended together, the lotus feet
of Lakshmi drawn on a pucca floor, the smell of ripe paddy
in the fields during the harvest season of Margasira. Om
Prakash had ceased to exist for him. So had the colliery and
the trade union. Samaru Khadia no longer existed, either in
memory or in oblivion.

Why had Pradyumna gone to the pithead meeting
today? He had never made much of politics. The way trade
unionists went on about exploitation, oppression, struggle,
and liberation! He never thought about these things. He
was from the middle class and felt whatever glory was his
came from that. The main reason for his unhappiness now
was that he had gone down from being middle class to
becoming a labourer, condemned to a repetitive and menial
job. Perhaps Pradyumna could have managed under the
alias of Samaru Khadia, but as Pradyumna Mishra he needed
at least the white-collar job of a tub checker. After all, he
was an educated graduate and observed the ritual of rolling
his sacred thread around his ear while attending to nature's
call, even if he did not carry out the more important task
of chanting the Gayatri mantra every evening. He did not
have the heart to endure the nightmare of working as a
casual loader, whose job was to load the tubs with coal like
an ordinary labourer.

Still, Pradyumna did go to the pithead meeting. He had
raised his hand to cast his vote in the union election, and his
name had been announced as a member of the executive
council of the about-to-be formed union. Worldly wise
as he was, Agani uncle had said, 'It's better to become a

member of the executive body. There's prestige in that. The officers will speak to you with respect. You will also be able to do what you need to.'

After hearing this Pradyumna felt he had been confirmed in his role as a labourer and no longer belonged to the middle class. Why did he feel this way? Almost everyone who had gained political capital belonged to the middle class. Had anyone by birth and upbringing a worker come forward to fight for the unity of the workers? It was people from the middle class who, with their own agendas, were asking workers to unite, and gaining mileage from that. The trade-union leaders were nothing but exploiters.

Om Prakash was a strange sort of person. Extremely naive, he hailed from somewhere in the north, either Uttar Pradesh or Bihar. Pradyumna had no idea whether he was middle class or working class, but there was some sort of rustic aggressiveness in the way he carried himself, as if he had lots of money. He was very jovial, behaving as if he had left behind acres of land on the banks of the river Ganga and valuable livestock—ten or fifteen dairy cows and buffaloes—and had condescended to reside in this state. It was as if he wanted to prove with every single word he uttered how unfavourably Odisha compared against his own state.

Pradyumna could not help but laugh at Om Prakash, but he appreciated the man's innocence. His way of speaking was rough and straightforward; the smallest provocation was enough to excite him. He did not know how to sweet-talk and never spoke softly. He boldly roamed about, clad only in an undershirt. He thought nothing of wearing a dhoti along with shoes and socks. He said that was the way he always dressed for festivals or special occasions. It was this innocence that touched Pradyumna. Who else could he count as a friend in this colliery?

Pradyumna could feel nothing but pity for the inhabitants of the colliery. Their worldview was limited to the coal mine and their own family. They did not have the slightest desire to know what was happening in the world outside, for instance about the hundreds of souls on any given street in any given city in America at this very moment. They had no ambition to star in a television serial, or to climb Mount Everest and plant the nation's flag at the peak. They could never imagine, even by mistake, going on a bicycle trip for a week or that one day bronze statues of themselves could be placed by the roadside or where streets met. They knew only about having sex, scrimping and saving, and the pleasures of the senses.

And the women in the colliery—their faces reflected how dull and lifeless they were, as though their life force had vanished, as if an invisible witch was sucking their blood through a straw every night and leaving them anaemic. Their whole lives were spent, day in and day out, amid wails, visits to the hospital, more wails, home, kitchen, the wailing of children suffering from fever and diarrhoea, and more visits to the hospital.

From such people, Pradyumna stood completely apart. Was it necessary for him to be like these complacent people? Perhaps he needed to leave all this behind and go someplace else.

But he was incapable of doing so. He was bound to remain in exile in this coal mine for the rest of his life. He was very soon going to become, like everyone else here, a man preoccupied with his own immediate surroundings. He would forget his own identity, the days of his childhood, adolescence, and youth. Pradyumna Mishra would slip out of his memory, leaving only Samaru Khadia behind. Such thoughts saddened him.

Om Prakash put down the glass of tea on the table with a thud and spoke in a whisper: 'Mishra, get up; let's leave. The situation here doesn't seem to be good.'

Pradyumna had no wish to leave. He did not feel like going anywhere really. And he absolutely did not want to return to the little hole that was Uncle Agani's quarters. He would not be able to stand the unwelcome presence of Runu and Jhunu. In his uncle's house he always felt as unwanted as a parasitic plant. No other house in the colliery had its doors open for him. He had had enough of loitering around aimlessly in the street. It was far better to while away some time at the tea shop. 'What's the matter? What do you think's wrong?' he asked.

'Look around; Members of the rival union are all around us. They look hostile. Something's about to happen.'

'What do you think'll happen?'

'C'mon, don't speak so loudly.'

Om Prakash walked up to the counter, dragging Pradyumna with him, paid for the tea, and stepped out. Before anyone knew what was happening someone called from behind, 'Hello Babu, listen. Come here for a minute.'

Pradyumna turned around to look, but Om Prakash had already caught hold of his hand and started to run. 'Run, run. Get away from here', he yelled. 'They're out to beat us up.'

Pradyumna turned back and saw two dark fat men racing towards them. He recognized them, but did not remember their names. He suddenly came back to his senses and realized their intentions were far from good. Before speeding up he saw Om Prakash running ahead of him. His heart was beating wildly as he ran behind Om Prakash, yelling, 'Help! Help!'

Before Pradyumna could move forward a step or two, someone caught him by the collar. His shirt was pulled against his neck and he almost choked. He looked at the face of the man who had pushed him to the ground and remembered he worked as a waggoner. Pinning Pradyumna down, the man said, 'So you're into trade unionism. Well, I'll soon have you cured of that.' He punched Pradyumna in the face and he blacked out. He felt excruciating pain in his face, nose, and mouth. It seemed as if his whole face had been set on fire. He thought he must be bleeding.

The other man shook the man who had beaten Pradyumna. 'He's not that important', he said. 'We've got to get Om Prakash. Let him go and come along.'

When the man overpowering him loosened his hold, Pradyumna pushed him away, got up and ran for his life towards the workers' quarters next to the road. There had been lots of activity in the area a little while earlier, with children playing and workers gossiping, stretched out on their rope beds. Now the children and the workers were nowhere in sight. Pradyumna saw that the ruffian was rushing towards him again while the other was running in the direction in which Om Prakash had fled. Pradyumna banged on a closed door out of sheer fright. 'Open the door, open up please. They're going to kill me.'

The door did not open. The thug was inching closer. Pradyumna was running out of time. He rapped on another door. It did not open either. He noticed a door a short distance away that was open a crack. He made a dash for it, but before he could get there, the door had been slammed shut.

He looked back and saw the man chasing him was rapidly advancing with a thick stick in his hand. Pradyumna realized that knocking on any more doors was futile. He had never had to face such a frightening situation. He was trying to think of a way to escape.

He had never taken part in any races nor had he ever joined an akhara. Once, when he was very little, he had played a game of football. There had been so much pain in his chest after it he had given up all strenuous games and exercises. No one had ever considered his thin rickety body a provocation for a fight. Had he ever imagined he would get involved in a brawl and get beaten up? He wiped away the blood running down his face. He felt no pain. He was so frightened he just kept running, oblivious to the people and the shops on the roadside, heedless of the cars and motorbikes.

He just kept running. When he came to his senses he found himself in his uncle's house. Runu, Jhunu, Peter, Uncle Agani, and his aunt sat around him.

His aunt was wiping the blood from his face and sobbing. Uncle Agani was fanning him with a hand fan even as he asked about what had happened. Peter, Runu, and Jhunu were speaking to each other in hushed voices. He was able to make out certain words in their conversation, words like 'union', 'Dhruba Khatua', and 'Ramachandra Mallick'. Pradyumna suddenly remembered the name of the person who had assaulted him was Ramachandra Mallick. He worked as a waggoner, and Pradyumna had seen him in Dhruba Khatua's office.

Pradyumna's nose hurt terribly. His head was reeling, his belly churning, and he felt nauseous. He could not keep his eyes open.

When he regained consciousness, night had fallen. Seated by his side, Jhunu was caressing his head. He immediately sat up. A grown girl sitting so close to him, in the presence of other people, was not acceptable to him. He could not bear such shamelessness. But in his uncle's house it was not uncommon to find the girls sitting close to men chatting with them intimately, flirting and snuggling with young men they barely knew or even those who were complete strangers. For Pradyumna, this was nothing to be proud of.

His nose and the space above his upper lip were burning. He was groggy and his head felt heavy. He could tell his face had been bandaged. Afraid that the police might find out,

Uncle Agani had called in a private doctor, who had put three stitches under Pradyumna's nose. This private doctor had charged thirty rupees and written out a prescription for medicine costing seventy-five rupees.

Om Prakash's arm had been broken in the fight. Uncle Agani had wanted to go and see him, but first his aunt and then Runu and Jhunu had stood blocking the door. Since the brawl was union related, he might be ambushed and set upon by Dhruba Khatua's gang.

Despite this, his uncle had managed to get out, shouting as he shoved the three of them out of the way. He was not yet back. His aunt was sobbing, lying on the bed hiding her face. Pradyumna felt like a criminal, as if he had upset the entire household.

He wondered about his uncle. He had called in a private doctor to avoid the complications of a police case, but had set out from home when he heard about Om Prakash's broken arm. He knew his uncle would go to the police station with Harishankar Babu to file a First Information Report.

Uncle Agani was definitely not a coward—he had not hidden in his house in this time of trouble. Why then had he wanted to keep Pradyumna away from the police? Was this a calculation on his part? As far as Pradyumna knew, his uncle could be clever but certainly not calculating. What could be the reason?

Pradyumna had absolutely no idea. But then, had he ever been able to fathom anyone's character? Had he been able to understand even his own? Is it ever possible to actually do that? Does anyone ever understand anyone else? Even after having known and seen oneself from birth one can suddenly be brought face to face with another side of one's own personality, the one lurking in the shadows. Only in an unguarded moment does this other side become visible.

When he sat down to eat, Pradyumna had a hard time opening his mouth. It was painful for him to chew. Jhunu tried to soften the rotis by soaking them in milk. She even tried to feed him, but stopped after he told her to. When he went to his room at the front of the house after taking his medicine, he noticed his bed had been made. It must have been Jhunu's work, he thought, since Runu tended to keep away from him. His aunt was still sprawled out on the bed face down, sobbing. So as not to be rebuked for causing the entire episode, he quietly went to bed. He could not fall asleep, but continued to lay in bed. Runu and Jhunu finished their meal as they talked. Awake, he eavesdropped. They called for his aunt to come and eat, and he heard her refuse from the bedroom. Runu and Jhunu washed the dirty dishes, fetched the things from the courtyard, and bolted the door. He saw and heard everything. Uncle Agani was still not home. The clock in the colliery police station struck eleven. His aunt was still on the bed, crying. He lay in bed trying to understand what was going on.

He was about to fall asleep when a sudden noise woke him up. Someone was trying to open the door. His aunt quickly got up to open it. Uncle Agani entered, and the strong odour of liquor filled the room. His aunt pressed a cloth to her nose. His uncle did not say anything odd or improper. Quietly, he crossed over to the courtyard. 'I won't eat anything', he said. 'Make my bed in the courtyard.'

Pradyumna felt sad. He remembered his village and home. No one in his family had ever touched liquor. If his father learned about his uncle's drinking he would probably ask Pradyumna to move out and live elsewhere. He might even insist Pradyumna quit his colliery job. Pradyumna felt sad, thinking that one day he too would become like his uncle. But did he aspire to be someone else? If so, who?

Pradyumna lapsed back into sleep as these thoughts ran through his mind. Late in the night he felt someone sleeping next to him. Who was it? In his uncle's two-room house his aunt and her son slept on the flat wooden bed in the bedroom, while the two sisters, Runu and Jhunu, slept on the floor, facing the wall. The bedroom and front room did not have a door separating them. Pradyumna slept on the rope bed in the front room.

Who was lying next to him? Minakshi? Pradyumna sat up with a start, completely awake. No, not Minakshi. Could it be Runu? Uncle Agani was considering getting her married to Pradyumna. Would the groom be Pradyumna or Samaru Khadia? Runu was very bashful but she had not exchanged a single word with Pradyumna until now. She slunk away at the sight of him. Could she have gotten into his bed, hoping something might happen? Pradyumna groped to find out who it was. It was not Runu.

Is it you, Jhunu?

I love you, Pradyumna Bhaina.

This isn't acceptable, Jhunu.

Why not?

This is sinful.

Why sinful?

If uncle and aunt learn of this, they'll be angry.

Don't worry about them, I know what they're worth. They can't pick on me.

What do you know about them?

Oh, nothing.

Tell me what you know.

Father keeps a woman from Chhattisgarh. And . . .

And?

Please don't tell anyone.

Jhunu moved closer to Pradyumna. She laid her head on his arm, her hot breath singeing his ears.

Sonu isn't my father's child.

How do you know?

I know. They used to have big fights earlier. Many in the colliery know about this.

Pradyumna was stunned. He broke into a cold sweat at the thought of such depravity. How murky things were here! 'No one loves you Pradyumna Bhaina, except me', continued Jhunu. 'The fondness father and mother show is only to get you to marry Runu. Don't you remember how mother resented your presence when you first came?'

Jhunu was lying next to him, her hand moving over his private parts. But his body was unresponsive. He was feeling strangled. Jhunu went on. 'Runu loves Peter; she's slept with him two or three times. Once I caught them. I know him too. You know what, Pradyumna Bhaina, you may marry Runu. I have no objection. Runu won't be able to marry Peter; father won't accept a son-in-law who's Christian. You may marry Runu. She won't object either. But I know this for sure, I love you, and will love you forever. Even if I too marry someone else, I will still love you.'

Could Pradyumna stop breathing? Jhunu was becoming restless. She was making unmistakeable advances towards Pradyumna. Uncle Agani would surely wake up from his sleep. 'Aren't you a man, Pradyumna Bhaina?' Pradyumna was feeling nauseous. Was his head reeling? Are you an imbecile, Pradyumna? Jhunu was trembling with excitement. Pradyumna's blood was heating up. The faces of his uncle, his aunt, father, and mother were receding from him. But Jhunu's presence was becoming larger and larger. What could Pradyumna say? How would he stem this tidal wave of sin? How? Minakshi, where are you Minakshi? Come and see how I'm sinking deeper and deeper into the quicksand of sin.

What! Why did Minakshi have to come to his mind at this time?

TEN

The constable took Harishankar inside the police station, seating him on a chair facing the Assistant Sub Inspector's desk. The officer's chair, covered in a white Turkish towel, was empty. On the desk lay some tan-coloured papers, along with a truncheon, a paperweight, and a telephone. A clock hung on the wall alongside the usual items: photos of the leaders of the nation, and the official calendar. The lock-up was on one side; it stood open, with no one inside. A mouse scooted across the cement floor. The constable asked him to stay seated, saying the officer was resting and would be informed of his visit upon waking.

This constable had been posted here recently; transfers happened often in the police department. If he had been there a few years earlier—before Dhruba Khatua came on the scene and when Harishankar had been the sole stand-in for Hema Babu—he would not have had the courage to keep Harishankar waiting simply because the officer-in-charge was taking a nap.

Was there no such thing as love or respect, then? Was everything done only out of fear? As long as you were in power everyone would salaam to you, but once you were powerless no one would show you the slightest respect. Take Hema Babu, now the object of so much reverence; he too had once dreaded the police. Who knew that better than Harishankar! How Hema Babu had gone underground when workers at the colliery had been locked out, and also during the Emergency—Harishankar had witnessed all this. Even an ordinary constable had been able to give Harishankar a mouthful then: Where's your deceitful Neta? There's a warrant out for him.

Yet when the same Hema Babu returned to power, many officers-in-charge, even the Deputy Superintendent, had busily fawned over him for as simple a favour as preventing a transfer. They went down before him on bended knee and sent basketfuls of fish to his first wife in the village. Harishankar has seen all of this. So in his mind he forgave the officer-in-charge for daring to not give him an audience today. He was prepared for anything and everything. Such things did not bother him anymore; his experience in trade-union politics had been long.

At first, Harishankar had not been very practical and was easily affected by taunts and sarcasm, flaring up at the slightest dig or jibe. Flattery overwhelmed him too. He was always worried about what people would think. It was Hema Babu who had taught him the ways of politics. The essence of what he had said was that there is no place in our democracy for the masses. They are nothing more than self-serving beings, devoid of ideals, of the power to reason, of conscience. Without any sense of the past or of the glorious heritage and history of this country, the masses only understand and work for their immediate interests. They are like a stream of water: it will run wherever you want it to, you just need a slope.

If that were not the case, would Hema Babu be winning all his elections? He had done nothing for his constituency; these days he did not even have the time to pay it a visit. The road to his village had not been paved. Nor did he have any time for the trade union of Tarbahar Colliery, which had jumpstarted his political career. It was never possible for anyone from the colliery to meet him in Bhubaneswar. Yet the union ran under his name. Dhruba Khatua's unlimited authority was backed by Hema Babu's power as a minister in the government. Tarbahar Colliery was his vote bank, his impregnable fortress.

Harishankar leaned against the back of the chair, staring at the ceiling and the empty lock-up. He eyed the tan-coloured files on the table. The Assistant Sub Inspector of this small outpost in Tarbahar Colliery, which served as a police station, was sleeping. The constable had taken off somewhere after having installed Harishankar on a chair. The crackling of the wireless radio could be heard in the adjoining room. Snatches of speech came floating in: 'Hello, hello 5-3-6 8 9-0-1. Hello, Black Pagoda calling. Over. Hello, hello. Note this down: 3-6-X M 9 P Q; P, P, P for Patna; PQ, JDC, B-3.' There was no one in the wireless room. The silence in the police station was palpable. The officer-in-charge was sleeping. The curtains on the door and the windows fluttered. As they blew apart, a grassless and walled patch of land became visible, a mynah its sole occupant. It looked solitary, and morose.

The officer made an entrance. Harishankar had dropped off to sleep while waiting. A strange habit of his, tension and stress brought him sleep. The chair creaked as the officer eased into it and the sound woke Harishankar up. Steadying himself in his chair, Harishankar greeted him. The officer did not so much as acknowledge this; he just smiled, a taunting smile. 'So what's new?' he asked. 'You're able to sleep so peacefully. What else is going on?'

Harishankar realized the officer had been informed about last evening's brawl. 'I came here looking for justice', he answered.

'Justice? You people start the fight and then look to us to deliver justice?'

'Start the fight? We didn't start it.'

The Assistant Sub Inspector was writing something in his notebook. He stopped and looked Harishankar in the face.

'If someone forces his way into your house, won't you put up a fight? Won't you hit him back?'

Harishankar sat up straight. 'Look here officer, trade unions aren't anyone's personal property. This is a basic right. You seem to have forgotten every worker has the right to decide which union he wants to join. We've formed a new one. It's been registered and is legal. We have a central committee at the all-India level, with branches in the various coal mines in India. Doesn't a national-level union have at least the right to try and recruit workers at

Tarbahar Colliery, provided of course the workers aren't pressured into joining?'

'Okay, imagine you were the secretary of the existing union and Dhruba Babu was trying to form another', replied the Assistant Sub Inspector. 'Wouldn't you protest?'

'It's quite understandable to protest, but should there be violence? There's a democratic way of protesting. What force can the union rely on other than the faith people place in it? Should that force be expressed through violence?'

The officer smiled. 'You're talking in abstractions; be practical. You've been in politics for a long time. You know as well as I do that non-violence, democracy, idealism—these are all just words, good to speak and good to hear. But in reality they're empty slogans. Is there a way to accurately measure what's democratic and what isn't? What's democratic for you may not necessarily be the same for me, and, besides, Mahatma Gandhi himself said that he didn't want the peace of the crematorium. If someone slaps you on one cheek, does non-violence oblige you to turn the other? Does it count as violence if you retaliate?'

Harishankar understood the officer would not take any action against Dhruba Khatua. He spoke with a slight edge to his voice. 'This means you're encouraging violence. You're an officer of the law, but you're talking as if you're a member of Dhruba Khatua's union. Taking sides like that does not suit someone in your position.'

The Assistant Sub Inspector stayed silent and tried to continue smiling. Harishankar could see that beneath the bold trappings of his police uniform this man was a coward.

Behind the cover of some flashy rhetoric, some quick retorts, the officer was insecure, willing to do anything to keep his job and his status. This person was a typical slave of a so-called democratic nation.

'If we were taking sides, would we have registered your First Information Report?' the officer asked. 'Why would we have filed a case?'

'You've filed a case? Under section 160, most likely, including both parties. There've been no arrests yet. Is that what you call filing a case? They came and assaulted us, and you've filed a case against us.'

The officer regained his aplomb. He smiled slyly. 'Who assaulted whom?' he asked. 'Dhruba Babu's party has filed a First Information Report stating your people assaulted his.'

'But you know that's not true. One person on our side has a broken arm. Another has seven or eight stitches on his face. You've filed a case against us based on their fake report.'

The officer leaned back against his chair. He took out his betel case from his pocket and put a paan in his mouth. Closing the case, he laid it on the table. 'What is true and what is fake?' he asked. 'Is there any way of proving truth or falsehood? Just as you've arranged your eyewitnesses, they've got theirs. So how can you be so certain your report is true and theirs is false?'

'So nothing is true or false? If one has power, one can pass off what is false as the truth. If that's how it is, where are our country, society, and morality headed?'

'Morality? Tell me truly, is there really such a thing? You've been in politics for a very long time and call yourself a Gandhian. But is there any trace of Gandhi's doctrine in your politics? Where do you find morality? In your lifestyle, in the administration, in the judiciary, or in the bureaucracy? 'Morality' is an antiquated word, found only in dictionaries. Tell me, is that not the case?'

Harishankar had never been very good at arguing or able to get the better of anyone through oratory or debate. Yet he believed there was a truth beyond arguments, a truth that one knew in one's heart. He did not want to prolong the dialogue, understanding it was pointless to do so. When confronted, the police officer was not going to back down. He got up, left the police outpost, and went out onto the street.

The streets, paan shops, hair salons, eateries, and vegetable markets of Tarbahar Colliery seemed to be throbbing with life. People eyed him suspiciously, keeping their distance. Harishankar could sense something was wrong. If he lingered, something bad might happen.

Harishankar started to lengthen his strides. Was he frightened? Tarbahar Colliery had been his empire once. But today? Where was this fear coming from? The people he had once fought for, whose dismissal he had agitated against during the era of the Company, whose service he had been instrumental in regularizing, whose suspension he had intervened to have revoked, whose wages had been reinstated despite going on strike—these people who had received his favours would not come out to help him now. Not even one would dare to come forward and say, 'We're with you Netaji. What do you worry or care about?'

Harishankar quickly returned home. It was almost ten o'clock. Today he would certainly arrive at the general manager's office late. Ghosh Babu, the senior clerk, was sure to make some snide remark. 'So you've decided to come Netaji. I thought you were skipping work today too.'

Harishankar was making an effort to go to the office regularly, but without much success. Firstly, it had become a habit not to go, and secondly, some or the other urgent chore would come up just when it was time to leave. At times, this had something to do with the union, and at others with a labourer seeking redress of some grievance.

Workers in charge of the trade union drew their salaries whether they went to work or not. This privilege had existed during the era of the Company and it became an unwritten standing order when the coal mine was nationalized. Although Harishankar had not been a part of the union for the past two years, he continued to enjoy the privilege. He was aware, of course, that his absenteeism irked many in the office, especially his colleagues.

A head clerk in the office of the personnel manager had once said to Harishankar: 'Your union leaders speak in such lofty terms about labour and labourers. You people glorify physical labour, yet you're reluctant to actually work. How come you don't encourage workers to increase production? On the contrary, when your interests are involved, you do everything you can to get workers to load tubs with minimum amounts of coal. You also encourage workers to avoid work. Marx and Engels, even Lenin and Mao, did not tell workers to do that. But in India, communists and non-communists alike push the idea it's possible to earn more and more while working less and less.'

Harishankar had babbled something in response just for the sake of argument, although he was bad at arguing. But he realized the clerk's words carried some truth. Even though he had not referred to Harishankar's absenteeism directly, Harishankar understood the thinly veiled barb directed against him, against his reluctance to work. From that day onward he decided he would go to the office regularly, even though no one would have confronted him if he hadn't. In the rare event someone did say something, his closeness to the general manager would prevent any harm coming his way. But Harishankar wanted the ideals he hoped would influence others guide his own character and conduct too.

He mentioned this to Agani Hota. 'Before taking on management, we have to be without fault. We have to tell our labourers not to skip work. We should not get involved when labourers ask for sick leave as an excuse not to work.'

Agani Hota had laughed off Harishankar's words. 'If we do that, can there be a union, Netaji? Will people care about us? What weight will we carry if we can't arrange a sick leave for someone when they need it? What if a person goes on leave without permission? If the manager doesn't allow him to come back to work he'll have to remain on leave without pay, reporting back only after a mark has been put on his record. He'll lose pay for fifteen or twenty days. He won't want that, will he? If we don't help him, then Dhruba Khatua will step in and win him over. Won't he join Dhruba Khatua's camp?'

'Well, Agani, many times you and Hema Babu have said that there's nothing called 'the masses', that 'the masses' are unable to think or remember.'

'Uh, Netaji, why aren't you being practical? I've simply said what anyone in this colliery would say. Everyone in the union is a politician. But the plain truth is that if we don't serve their personal interests they'll turn against us.'

'But I don't understand, Agani. What sort of self-contradictory doctrine is this?'

'You have so much experience, Netaji. You've been involved in trade unions for the past thirty years. I'm just a baby compared to you. What can I tell you? Don't you know what you want, what 'the masses' are, how they behave, and what they want.'

In fact, what was meant by 'the masses' remained a mystery for Harishankar. At every step he was being torn apart by contradictions. What appeared right at one moment turned out to be wrong the next. Why was it like that? Harishankar's views were never firmly grounded in theory. He lacked self-confidence. Hadn't his long experience resulted in understanding or wisdom?

Harishankar reached home. His house was an untidy mess. He had left his official quarters after being shifted to the office of the general manager, although he did not have to do that. Hema Babu had warned him at the time, 'Why are you giving up your official accommodation? I can get your transfer cancelled if you'd like.'

Harishankar had put in no effort to prevent his transfer or to stay in his quarters: the trade union was at the forefront of his thoughts. He knew the transfer would not make him start going to the office once again. Besides, in a sense, and no matter if he was posted in the general administration of the colliery or in the store or in the office of the general manager, he did not have to go to the office on a regular basis. What remained were his domestic duties. He had never given priority to home and family; having a roof over his head had been enough.

His mother sat leaning against the wall on the front veranda. Had she been crying as she looked up at the sky? Had the tears that had rolled down dried on her cheeks? What could she have been crying about? Was she aggrieved? Harishankar had never given much thought to anyone in his family. Maybe this is what had caused his wife, Tarangini, to have a mental breakdown. She wandered about here and there. Earlier he had not even known what his sons Kuna and Runa were up to, what classes they were in, whether they studied. After he was finished with union work, he got to know that Runa had failed his college examinations two years earlier and that Kuna had left his studies long ago. When Hema Babu freed him of his obligations to the union, Harishankar started paying attention to his family. He stayed home most of the time, took an interest in the affairs of Runa and Kuna, and chatted happily with Tarangini. Her aimless wandering and craziness came to an end. She slept well at night, mopped the floor every day, and did the laundry regularly. She had cleared a patch in front of the house where she grew greens. She even insisted on getting a pressure cooker to make it easier to cook meat. Now that Harishankar was becoming re-immersed in union affairs her craziness returned. The old sleeping pills were ineffective. These days Harishankar returned home at midnight. His mother would crawl out to give him his meal, blabbering on about the difficulties and hardships of life, Tarangini's madness, Runa and Kuna's waywardness, all as he sat and ate. He listened distractedly, pretending to be paying attention, nodding his head and saying yes. In reality, however, his head was full of matters relating to the union and management, Dhruba Khatua, Mr Mishra, Deshmukh, and the office of the general manager. He let his mother's words go in through one ear and out the other.

His mother sat against the wall, looking up at the sky. Seeing Harishankar, she got up with a start. This habit women had—Tarangini too had it—repelled Harishankar. His wife used to panic the moment Harishankar set foot in the house. Women never thought about the mental strain the person returning home might be under. Annoyed, he asked, 'Aah, why're you acting like that?'

At this his mother burst into a flood of tears. 'I had to witness such misery because of my bad luck', she said as she continued to cry. 'Did I give birth to all of you and take such pains to make men of all of you only to see a day like this?'

Harishankar was annoyed. 'Tell me what happened. Why are you acting up so much?'

'Has there been something so earth shaking it bears telling? It's my luck that has gone awry.'

Harishankar became angry. 'Say what you have to say. Don't make me angry. I'm already feeling out of sorts. Don't talk nonsense.'

His mother calmed down a little and stopped crying. 'I haven't had a sip of tea all day', she complained. 'There isn't even a handful of rice in the house. The daughter-in-law's raving mad. Runa and Kuna haven't been seen since this morning.'

'Where have they gone? Why haven't you asked someone to go out and get food?'

'Is there enough money in the house to send someone out on an errand? Even after your father became a sanyasi I didn't face such hardship. Son dear, does your mother have to undergo such distress and pain just for a handful of rice?'

His mother could barely suppress her tears, and, in the end, they flooded out as if a dam had burst. She had taken a lot of trouble to raise him and get him to stand on his own two feet. His father had given up the world to become a sanyasi when Harishankar was little, and he only remembered his bearded face, with its halo of long matted hair tied up on the top of his head.

Once his father had come and stood beneath the thatched eaves at nightfall. His mother had stood leaning against the wall, wiping away her tears with the end of her sari. She told Harishankar to go and touch his father's feet.

Harishankar had not wanted to show him respect, but still he went forward and bowed. 'This is Hari', said his mother.

'He's grown so big.' Father gave a charming smile. 'I'd thought he'd be much smaller. Where's Rabi?'

As always, his father had left again after stopping by briefly. Every time his father left, his mother would sprawl out on the mattress, bury her face in the pillow, and sob. Even now Harishankar could hear those sobs echo in his heart. He had never learned to love his father, but somewhere in his arteries flowed his father's blood. His mother said Harishankar took after him—the same face, the same eyes. He had also turned out like his father—detached, unconcerned, without desire—and it was precisely these qualities that made Harishankar unable to love him.

One evening his father had come calling. He took Harishankar with him. While walking in the open expanse of the village Harishankar could feel the touch of his father's hand on his back. His father was telling him, 'Look son, you're grown up now. It'll be up to you to run the household. I'm off to the Himalayas; God is calling for me. I've no wish to be mired in illusion and desire, but it's not easy to snap the cord of illusion. Despite being a sanyasi my mind keeps getting drawn back to the world. No longer. Time isn't on my side. I know you've not been able to like me, but do try to understand me. I'm sure you'll be able to forgive me if you can understand me. Anyway, I'm leaving the home and family in your hands. Look after your mother. Rabi has to study. Your mother's very unfortunate. I haven't been able to make her happy. Try and do that.'

As he spoke these last few words, his father had choked up and his eyes had moistened. He had proceeded towards the village fields, while Harishankar remained standing in the shadows. His father soon faded into the distance. Harishankar was tearless. Had he grieved? Was he angry? He had no idea what he had thought. Back home he found his mother had stopped crying; she had checked herself. She called him inside and made him sit on a mat. By the light of the lantern he saw determination in his mother's eyes. And as if on cue, much of the confidence of the high-school, first-division scoring Harishankar had come surging back. He knew it was up to him now. He had suddenly become an adult. To his mother's question, 'How will we run the house?' he had replied, 'I'll go to work.'

The sound of his own voice had surprised Harishankar. Where was so much confidence coming from, with such a thundering voice? Who had given him such strength? Who had inspired him to believe in himself? 'Aren't people from our village employed in the colliery? I'll go there in search of a job.'

His mother had arranged for twenty rupees by pawning her meagre jewellery. A new chapter had begun. But that was thirty or thirty-five years ago. Where had Harishankar lost that sense of responsibility? After he got a job in Tarbahar Colliery he had slowly started gravitating towards the union. In the process he began to forget his home and family, his sense of duty, and commitments. Perhaps his father's blood ran through him still. For this reason, despite his dislike of his father, he had grown detached and disaffected towards home and family. Pretty much as his father had.

'There isn't even a rupee in the house. Who will I stretch out my hand to? I can't see very well. At this age I burn my hands cooking, and I'm without food in my belly most days.'

Harishankar went into the house and took out his passbook from the wooden almirah. Last month he had had only thirty-five rupees left, but this month's salary of two thousand four hundred rupees must have been deposited by now. He had forgotten to draw some cash. He put the passbook in his pocket. He had only one rupee in his pocket and did not know which shop would let him buy groceries on credit and which shops to avoid. Which one would oblige him now? He had never bought groceries in his entire life.

He went outside and spoke to his mother. 'I'll have vada and samosa sent over. Manage with that during the day, and this evening I'll withdraw money from the bank and buy rice.'

He said this and left without waiting to hear her reply. It was as if he lacked the courage to face her. What if his mother asked him what had happened to the assurances he had given on the day his father had bidden his final farewell and gone on his way? What would Harishankar's answer be?

Once he was out on the street the old worries came racing back. What had Harishankar got from so many years of working in the trade union? Money, riches, real estate, a ministership? Were any of these what he really wanted? Perhaps not. He had buried all his hopes and aspirations, successes and failures under the heady feeling of accomplishing something important. The excitement came from being caught up in the throes of doing this or that, of unfolding events. Could this be called self-interest? Why was it then that everyone was so intent on denying the existence of idealism and morality? Don't they exist? What had Harishankar lived on then? What had supported him until today? Why had he sacrificed his home and family, happiness and peace, duties and obligations at the altar of the union?

When Harishankar came to Bhaina's eatery, it was rush hour and Bhaina was sitting behind his counter reading a newspaper. He ordered six samosas and six vadas to take home and asked for two fried potato patties and half a cup of tea for himself. His mother was not fond of potato patties; she was very picky. Six samosas and six vadas—surely his mother would not be able to eat all of those. But it was better to get them. Who knew if Tarangini or Runa and Kuna would not turn up, starving? Harishankar used to run a tab at this eatery.

Bhaina stopped reading his newspaper, got up, and came and sat on a chair opposite Harishankar. The waiter—a young boy—placed a plate of patties and chutney in front of him. Bhaina moved forward a little and spoke softly, 'Netaji, I have something I want to say.'

As he struggled to break the patties into smaller pieces with a spoon, Harishankar asked, 'What is it?'

'Netaji, you owe me six hundred rupees so far this month alone. Last month's total was three hundred.'

Setting aside the spoon and lifting a patty from the plate, Harishankar asked in utter surprise, 'What? Six hundred for this month?'

'And the month's not over yet. Isn't the kitchen being used at home, Netaji? Please don't get me wrong, but these are bad signs, of a person deserted by Lakshmi. I've wanted to tell you many times, but couldn't bring myself to do it.'

'Snacks for six hundred rupees? Who's been ordering them?'

'What do you mean who's been ordering them? Your son, your wife, your old mother — whoever can. The bill adds up to twenty rupees a day. Netaji, please put some limits on the people at home. That's a lot of snacks.'

Harishankar looked serious. His world was falling to pieces, and he had to assume responsibility for that. It was his duty to raise Runa and Kuna to be successful in life, but he justified his neglect of home and family by his dedication to a noble cause. But what was that noble goal? Did he even have one? And if he did, what gave him the right to ruin the lives of his mother, his wife, and his sons, in the futile pursuit of an elusive goal, no matter how grandiose it might seem.

As he was leaving the eatery after collecting the package of vadas and samosas from the boy, Harishankar told Bhaina, 'Well, let me look into the matter; I'll make enquiries at home. For now, don't stop putting things on the tab. I'll get back to you after two or three days.'

Harishankar looked at his watch. Fifteen minutes past eleven. God, it was late! He had to get to the general manager's office, seven or eight kilometres away. Who knew if he would be lucky enough to catch a bus right away?

When Harishankar turned towards his house, he heard someone calling from behind, 'Netaji, Netaji.'

Harishankar turned around. It was Agani, on a bicycle. He must have come directly from the pit; his shorts and shirt, his entire body, were bathed in soot. He had his helmet on.

When he got close to Harishankar, Agani jumped off the cycle. 'Great news, Netaji.'

'What news?'

'The project officer's been transferred.'

'For real?'

'The message just arrived. The general manager had telexed a report to the head office about the brawl the other day. There's been a reply.'

Harishankar had never imagined victory would come so soon. He handed the package of snacks over to Agani.

ELEVEN

What had Deshmukh imagined would happen? That a grand celebration would mark such an occasion? That a trumpet would resound as he took possession of his realm? That the little world of this coal mine would be upended by the sound of a bugle? The trees and the plants, the entire population, the coal-loaded tub, the rush of the conveyor belt with its mechanical whir, the siren at eight in the morning, and the whistle of the night watchman in the middle of the night—weren't these too supposed to be transformed? Hadn't his horoscope predicted he would gain dominion over this fabled land?

Yet nothing of the sort came to pass. The news reached Deshmukh at ten that a telex had been delivered to the general manager's office. He tried calling the office, but was unable to get through. He looked for his jeep, but there was no fuel. Had there not been this problem, then the driver would not have showed up, and had there not been a problem with the driver, then the battery would have been dead. So Deshmukh did nothing, did not stir. He stayed put in his office, randomly thumbing through the pages from books, technical magazines, sketches, and the book detailing safety rules for the coal mine. He did not bother his typist, did not call Anita, did not scold his driver. He did not put a call through to the foreman of the auto section or to the engineer, to requisition another vehicle. He simply sat quietly in his office.

Anita broached the subject when he returned home for lunch, asking if he was going to be promoted or if someone else would be.

'Who knows?' he responded nonchalantly.

'Why haven't you asked the general manager or the personnel manager? Why haven't you sent a telex to head office? Didn't you say you know a certain Deotale sahib at head office?'

'Who knows?'

'What do you mean 'who knows'? You're always being secretive, aren't you? You always bury things deep inside you and don't share anything with your wife. Look at the other officers. They fill their wives in on everything— which subordinate's taking leave, who's doing overtime, who's toadying up to whom. You're the only one who tries to prove how strong he is by not sharing any information with his wife.'

This was how their dinner-table conversation had gone. By bedtime Deshmukh had grown quite tense, but for no specific reason. He could have opened up to Anita, but he chose to keep quiet. He felt the fatigue would unbearably weigh him down if he told her everything in the minutest detail. Better to focus on the prospects and promises these moments held, better to imagine them, to turn them over in his mind. That would be the best way to forget for the time being.

Anita chose not to needle Deshmukh when she saw how serious he had become. Deshmukh had, of course, called Anita from his office to convey the news to her first, though Anita was not home then to take the call. When he returned to work after lunch he knew the news had spread through the entire office. The office superintendent came and offered his congratulations; the ever-defiant watchman of the deputy chief mining engineer gave him a long salute; the clerks who had never showed him any respect seemed cowed.

A jeep stood ready with a tank full of diesel to take him to the general manager's office. The driver was waiting. The faulty phone line had been repaired. Everything was now going the way it should, now that the planetary curse afflicting him had been lifted. What he had hoped for had come true, though not entirely unexpectedly. Mr Mishra was not in his office. Deshmukh waited outside the door. The watchman threw it open so he could make a grand entry. The floor was covered in an expensive carpet. The air cooler whirred ever so softly as it blew in cool air. The soft colour of the costly distemper on the wall glimmered in the light. The fragrance from the room freshener wafted across the room. The chair of deputy chief mining engineer was waiting for him.

Was victory within his grasp already? But then how cold, unexciting, and lifeless it felt! This much-coveted chair! How weary, stale, and flat it now seemed! He returned to his former office and phoned Anita. His voice sounded quite calm, as if nothing special had happened. Or nothing more important than when the croton plant in his garden had died and he had asked for its replacement, without regard for what Anita might say about it. Or maybe it was as if he was absent-mindedly asking Anita to change the milkman because she had complained he was mixing water in the milk. He spoke in his characteristic non-committal tone: 'Anita, Mr Mishra has received his marching orders. I'm being put in charge of his department.'

'You're being promoted!' Anita responded gleefully. Deshmukh returned the phone to the cradle without reacting to her happiness. He surveyed his office once again. It was dull, flat, ordinary. A table with some files and a paperweight, three chairs, a steel almirah, a telephone—that was all. How could one possibly warm to such a place? But then, suddenly, a craving for his old office flashed through his mind, working its way through the deadened and paralyzed anthill of his feelings. Such impractical sentiments! A shame really!

All of this had taken place three days ago. And then the morning Deshmukh took up his new position—was it different from any other? The steno who came to wish him good morning, the head clerk who brought him files, the workers who came to ask for advances on their wages, the person who came to submit the raising report for the mines, the overseer countersigning the bills of the contractor in charge of construction work, the headmaster responsible for convening the next board meeting of the school management committee, the storekeeper who came to ask for advice on whether or not to purchase replacement materials for the store locally or to requisition them from the central store, the engineer who came to tell him servicing of the office vehicles was due—all of them looked at him as if they were used to seeing him in this chair from time immemorial, as if there was nothing new, as if nothing at all had changed. It was as though Deshmukh had always been in this chair.

On the day of the farewell meeting, Deshmukh and Mr Mishra shook hands. At that moment, he felt relieved of all his feelings of inferiority. Holding Mr Mishra's hand firmly and puffing out his chest, he said with a smile, 'Wish you good luck.' At that moment he felt like Napoleon Bonaparte, with Mr Mishra reduced to a vanquished emperor now being pardoned out of pity. Otherwise, he would have given Mr Mishra a tongue lashing in his farewell speech. But he did not say anything. Nor did he try to avoid the chores related to Mr Mishra's transfer. Without hesitating, he arranged for Mr Mishra's personal effects to be packed and agreed to provide a truck. He had also released a few workers from the main shift to help with the move.

Deshmukh was now safely ensconced on his cherished throne, but nothing seemed to have changed. Was all this really a sign his life had turned around? When? How? Yet what about the slights, the stress, and the struggles he had endured for so many years? Had he simply been deluding himself? Surely they had really existed. And yet it seemed to him the old chair, the old office, and the hassle-free earlier phase of his life had been better, as if it was more desirable to live as a man without qualities, as just one officer among many.

Deshmukh came out of the office and stood in the doorway. The peon hurriedly sprang to his feet. The driver, standing away from the jeep and lost in gossip, came running towards the jeep. The watchmen at the gate straightened up.

Today was payday, and so the main gate to the office was closed. There were people and noise everywhere. Earlier, officers of the rank of deputy chief mining engineer would not have shown up on payday, wanting to avoid scenes of drunken workers filled with Dutch courage showing off by hurling abuse at officers. No deputy chief mining engineer had wanted to court the trouble of being put in a fix or being publicly ridiculed.

When he first began to work in the coal mines, Deshmukh had been struck by its strange antisocial society, a world completely different from that of small-town Jalna in Maharashtra. All colliery societies were alike in their values, culture, and consciousness, different from purely residential townships. Drinking and sex scandals were common. Of course, Deshmukh had noticed a change in this world over the last few years. The rate of drinking had gone down slightly; people were not as eager to get involved in drunken street fights. In the past the sound of quarrelling, fighting, and crying would float in from the workers' colony on pay days. At first this had been replaced, Deshmukh had observed, by cheap songs from smutty Hindi movies played over loudspeakers, and these days even this had stopped, since all the houses in the workers' colony now had television sets and doors in the colony were shut tight by nightfall.

The people of the colliery were addicted to movies and loved to imagine themselves as characters in films. But the reels were not real. Had they been, Deshmukh's story would have ended here, and he would have become a statue of a man standing like the hero at the end of a successful film. But it didn't turn out that way. Deshmukh suddenly saw Dhruba Khatua. He pushed the gate open and barged in, his face livid with rage. The watchman, far from stopping him, was saluting.

Deshmukh had never liked Dhruba Khatua. He believed people like Khatua were the products of a decadent culture. Khatua had never given him any quarter during Mr Mishra's heyday, but had come running to congratulate him on his promotion. Acting as if he was overwhelmed with gratitude, he had said: 'Sir, we're always on the side of management. We'll vilify you in public, but please don't feel bad about that. You know how people are; they can't be controlled unless management is called names. But you'll come to no harm as long as I'm around, of that I can assure you.'

That day Deshmukh got a proof of how cunning a man can be and how he can shamelessly try to advance his own agenda, with a smile on his face. He was amazed; goose pimples popped up all over his body out of contempt. Nevertheless, he used honeyed words and shook hands with

Khatua. He had even ordered tea and discussed mine related issues with him.

Dhruba walked up to Deshmukh and greeted him. He seemed to be the picture of sweetness, the anger previously on his face had disappeared. Dhruba greeted him effusively and with a beaming smile. 'Sir, I'd like to have a word with you. It's urgent.'

'Come on in', said Deshmukh as he entered his room. Dhruba Khatua followed behind. Deshmukh sat in his chair, leaning back in it. He rang the bell for the peon and ordered two cups of tea. Making himself comfortable in his swivel chair, turning a little first to left and then to right, he asked, 'So what's it you want to talk about?' Khatua reassumed his earlier form, his face turning red in anger. 'Have you permitted Harishankar's union to recruit members?' he asked.

Deshmukh had known something like this would happen. Before taking up his new position he had made the decision to allow the new union to form. He had already thought about how to deal with Dhruba Khatua and his followers if they demanded an explanation. He smiled slightly. 'First drink your tea. We'll talk later.'

Dhruba Khatua was about to lift the teacup but then thought of something and put the cup down. 'No, I want an answer first', he said. 'Have you issued an order allowing members to be signed up?'

Deshmukh had given the matter a good deal of thought the night before. It was not that he had a soft spot for Harishankar Patnaik's union, but it was true the union had played a role in his promotion. He knew no union was intent on improving the lot of the workers, that everyone was busy promoting their own self-interest. Harishankar or Dhruba Khatua, they were all cast from the same mould. The workers alone could help themselves. The union was an utter delusion, a lie.

Besides, how could he easily forget the slight and neglect people like Dhruba Khatua had shown to him during Mr Mishra's time? How could he possibly be nice to these people? He had given the matter a lot of thought. Sentimentality would not suit him now. A wrong step on his part would be as disastrous for him as it had been for Mr Mishra.

Harishankar must enjoy some popular support, just as Dhruba Khatua did. If not, would people have attended his meeting at the pithead in such large numbers? So Deshmukh ought to stay on the good side of both of them, so that neither would suspect him of backing the other. Smiling he said, 'I've only asked them to collect dues from recruited members; I haven't called them over here about the police case, Dhruba Babu. Besides, I've asked them to stay at least one hundred meters away from the pay counter. Your group has the privilege of being closest to the counter. What do you have to be afraid of if you have the people's support? If people leave you and cross over to his side, then that would only reveal your loosening hold over them. I believe you enjoy the trust of the workers of Tarbahar Colliery even now. Collecting dues shouldn't be a problem for you.'

Dhruba Khatua stood up and pushed back his chair. 'Sir, permitting Harishankar to collect money wasn't a good decision. And as for the support of the workers? Very soon you'll see if people are behind us. In fact, we'll show you today. But you'll be responsible for what happens.'

'Are you threatening me?'

Dhruba Khatua was on his way out. He stopped and turned around. 'This is politics, sir, and threats have no place in politics. There's only room for action. I'm saying you should bring out a new notice saying only the recognized union is authorised to collect dues. You'll see how we'll drive them out as soon as the notice is out. Look sir, you're in a position where you've got to consider all the angles before making a decision.'

'Please don't try and tell me what I should or shouldn't be doing. I know what I have to do.'

'You're not going to issue a new notice then.'

'No.'

'Fine, then don't blame me for what happens.'

On his way out, Dhruba Khatua slammed the door, as if delivering a stinging slap. Deshmukh felt terribly insulted. He heard Dhruba Khatua call him names, standing outside. He knew from his years of experience in the colliery that such name-calling was nothing new.

At the beginning he had thought such flare-ups had something to do with class consciousness and class struggle, but now he realized all this was a farce, all part of the game of politics. These days he tended to ignore such things. Still, he could not help but feel depressed. What would

the peon have thought of Dhruba Khatua's slamming the
door shut? He pressed the bell and told the peon when
he arrived, 'Tell the watchman to show Khatua Babu out
through the gate.'

The peon's nervous smile told Deshmukh he did not
have the courage to carry out the order. The peon, a bundle
of nerves, left without a word. Deshmukh felt a rush of
blood to his ears; his feet were shaking; his heart thudding.
He drank some water. No, he did not care about Dhruba
Khatua's threats, but why had the fellow slammed the door
as he left? What would the peon think?

Deshmukh rang up Mr Mirchandani, the general
manager. 'Sir, this is Deshmukh speaking.'

'Go ahead.'

'Sir, Dhruba Khatua has just been in my office. He
came to threaten me.'

'Dhruba Khatua? Why?'

'Because I've permitted Harishankar Patnaik to sign up
workers, a hundred yards away from the pay counter.'

'What? You gave Harishankar permission? Who asked
you to do that?'

Deshmukh's bubble burst. It was Mr Mirchandani who
had gotten him to teach Mr Mishra and Dhruba Khatua a
lesson by lending support to Harishankar. Had he forgotten
that? Deshmukh didn't know what to say, other than, 'I
thought Harishankar had your backing, sir.'

Mr Mirchandani blew up. 'What are you talking
about? I'm managing such a huge organization. What
possible interest could I have in union politics? And who is

Harishankar Patnaik anyway? Look Deshmukh, don't try to blame me for the mess you've made.'

Deshmukh's world darkened. Never before had he felt so insecure, frightened, and weak. His own voice sounded strange to him. 'Sorry sir, I've made a mistake.'

'Mistake! Do you think it's just a simple mistake? Do you know how this mistake will turn out? Let me tell you you'll be responsible for any loss or harm done to the unit.'

What a strange position he was in! It was well known that Mr Mirchandani could not stand Mr Mishra for the simple reason the latter had been indulging Dhruba Khatua. And now he was turning against Deshmukh precisely because Dhruba Khatua was not being humoured by Deshmukh. What exactly did Mr Mirchandani want?

'Come over to the office immediately', ordered Mr Mirchandani. 'We'll discuss the matter in detail here.'

Deshmukh hung up and pressed the bell. He told the peon to ask the driver to get ready. Then he went to the bathroom. It belonged to him alone. It smelled good, was sparkling clean, and carpeted. The commode was on one side and a wash basin and urinal were on the other. There was a mirror on the wall above the wash basin. Deshmukh used the urinal and then washed his face with a little soap. He dried his face and combed his hair with the comb he kept in his pocket. He tried to look as calm as possible, hiding his inner turmoil. This is what is called having 'personality'. The more you repress your feelings, the more you conceal your inmost thoughts, the more you are considered to have a strong personality.

Mr Mirchandani surely had some liking for him. Why else would he have called him to his office soon after his promotion to give him some tips? These could amount to a small book with the title 'How to become an effective officer'.

'The more you show yourself to be quick to anger and serious', Mr Mirchandani had told him, 'the more your stock will rise. Even if you're pleased with someone, make it a point not to show it. Never say 'yes' to anybody on any matter. Never grant a request for leave, or for an advance on salary, or for use of the office jeep the first time round. If you do, the person who has benefitted will feel that, far from receiving a favour, he got something he was entitled to. If you oblige him after putting him off a few times, then he'll feel grateful. He'll feel that despite being a tough officer you have a soft spot for him.'

Once, Deshmukh had attended a nine-day programme in Hyderabad, an intensive training course for managers in coal mines across the country. He still remembered what the instructor had said in one of the sessions: a good manager never says 'no'; his main job is to get his staff to deliver. Don't ever say 'no' to someone who shows up late for work or who applies for leave or who asks to be absent half a day. You have the right not to grant him leave and to make him be present in the office, but he probably won't do any work; he'll lose the taste for it. On the other hand, if you grant him leave on the condition he complete his work at a later date without charging overtime, then you'll see you've been able to get a lot out of him.

Deshmukh had shared the story with the general manager. Mr Mirchandani had laughed it off. 'All that is pure theory, without any practical value whatsoever. The truth is, if you give someone a little room, he'll try to find a way to get more. Don't you know the Indian mindset? It's made up of opportunism, laziness, and selfishness. You think you can sweet-talk someone into completing his work and that person will do it? Never. He's not going to deliver as long as he hasn't been forced to. There's only one way in this country to get work done. The greater the distance you maintain from your subordinates, the better. Discover your inferiors' weak points and strike them hard there. Always find fault with your inferiors and charge them with non- or poor performance. Create an atmosphere where work is everything and nothing else matters. Then you'll see how everyone has their tails between their legs and are doggedly engaged in their work.

Deshmukh came out of the bathroom. The peon was on his feet in a flash. This peon had never had one iota of respect for him while Mr Mishra ruled the roost, yet how obediently he stood today! Deshmukh went out and got into the jeep.

Mr Mirchandani was always telling him to be firm, as firm as possible. Had Deshmukh been weak up until now? Hadn't he learned yet to assert his officer-like personality? Or was it that he remained stuck in his earlier image of himself as neglected and powerless, an officer in name only? Was Dhruba Khatua's misbehaviour today a challenge to his authority?

What should Deshmukh do now? Should he confront Dhruba? No, he could not do that because the general manager would not stand for any kind of worker unrest. Besides, what was the point of cultivating Harishankar? Who was he anyway? A union leader with ambition. There was no difference between Dhruba Khatua and him; they were two sides of the same coin. Did the workers stand to make gains because of either of them? Deshmukh leaned back in his seat. The general manager would surely find a solution. After all, he was in his boss's good books.

At 4 p.m. the news reached Deshmukh that the second shift had stayed away from work in response to a sudden strike call. Mr Naidu, the manager in charge now, had called to break the news.

'What are they demanding?'

'Don't have a clue, sir. It'd be good if you came over.'

Anita was with him when this happened. It was just after his siesta and before he went back to the office. He had not yet had his tea. Anita was mixing a sugar cube into it. 'Who was on the phone?' she asked. 'What's the matter?'

'It seems the workers have suddenly stopped working. The reason isn't clear; I have to go.'

'Are you going to the pithead on pay day? Most of the people will be tipsy. And on top of that, there's worker unrest. There's no telling what'll happen.'

'Anita, our work is managing the workers, and I'm in charge of the colliery. Would it look good if I sit back when there's a strike in my unit?'

Deshmukh got dressed and gulped down his tea standing up. Hurriedly, he put on his safety shoes in place of the dress shoes Anita had taken out, thinking he might need to go underground. He left.

The pit area was crawling with people. Two security guards came running to cordon him off from the crowd. At first Deshmukh was scared to see so many people, but he did not let on he was afraid. He indicated to the guards, standing near him with their sticks raised, that everything was okay and there was nothing to worry about. They escorted him through the crowd into the office.

In the office was Mr Naidu, visibly worried. Other junior managers and engineers stood close by. The under managers and the mining sardars surrounded the desk. On seeing Deshmukh, Mr Naidu got up from where he was sitting and moved to another chair. 'Hope there was no problem in coming here, sir', he said. 'Today's payday. People are drunk, and you never know what might happen.'

'What's the matter?' asked Deshmukh. 'Why aren't the workers going into the mine?'

'This isn't their own doing. Dhruba Babu's men aren't letting anyone go down.'

'Why not? Why're they acting like hooligans? How can one group threaten the workers to make them stay away from work, and how can such threats work?'

'The reason no one's going down is because they're afraid. Moreover, today's payday; many people don't show up for work on payday. People aren't generally in the mood to work. On top of all that, who would want to go to work and get into trouble?'

'Did you have a chat with the union people?'

'The Dhruba Babu group can't be reached. I talked with Agani Hota, who's part of Harishankar's group. Even they can't make sense of the strike.'

'Does that mean the strike wasn't called by the union?'

Mr Naidu lowered his head for a while and then answered. 'The truth is it was Dhruba Khatua's men who got the workers not to go into the pit, but now they don't want to be in the picture.'

'Why not?'

A mining sardar spoke up. 'Sir, let me say something. Why are all of you talking as if you don't know what's going on? All of you know this strike has been masterminded by Dhruba Khatua. You've allowed Harishankar Patnaik's men to recruit members. That's why there's a strike.'

Deshmukh looked sternly at the mining sardar. He wondered if this man was on Dhruba Khatua's side. Who could say? 'Can that be why there's a strike? Without giving notice? Where's the list of demands? Where's the one-month notice?'

'As far as a list of demands goes, a thousand and one can be produced immediately. And about one month's notice, well that's why Dhruba Khatua's men haven't come forward. That means they haven't officially called a strike but want to show how powerful they are.'

Deshmukh thought it wise not to cross words with the mining sardar. With a wave of his hand, he motioned him to stop and the foreman and the other mining sardars present there made this person be quiet. Someone dragged him outside. 'Hang up a notice', Deshmukh told Mr Naidu, 'saying the workers engaged in illegal strike action will face a week's pay cut as per the standing order of Coal India.'

'May I say something, sir?' Mr. Naidu asked. 'I know from experience this kind of notice does more harm than good. If those who called the strike can stop workers from showing up for one day of work, then the strike will continue for one week. The workers know about the rule of a week's pay cut whether they stop work for one day or a week. So who'd want to work for a full week when the result's the same?'

What choice did Deshmukh have? Should he file a report with the police? Should he call Harishankar Patnaik and ask him to deal with the strikers? Or should he call Dhruba Khatua and tell him he was ready to accept his terms and conditions? What should he do?

Suddenly he remembered Mr Mirchandani. He had forgotten to inform the head of the organization of the matter. Only that afternoon he had been cautioned by Mr Mirchandani that Dhruba Khatua was dangerous and had to be taken in hand. When Deshmukh entered Mr Mirchandani's office, he found him to be unexpectedly calm. There was absolutely none of the irascibility he had shown on the phone earlier, either in his tone of voice or his appearance. He kept Deshmukh waiting for a long time. Deshmukh sat and drank his tea, while Mr Mirchandani pored over files and signed them. At last he lifted his head and asked, 'So you had a faceoff with Dhruba Khatua today?'

Deshmukh was taken aback by the general manager's words. He had expected Mr Mirchandani to flare up the moment he entered his office and give him a good dressing down. But the general manager remained surprisingly calm as he asked the question.

'Have I gone wrong somewhere, sir?'

'Look, Deshmukh, Tarbahar Colliery falls under your jurisdiction; it's not for me to meddle in your work. You're the person taking decisions about what's happening here, both the good and the bad, about local police matters and the like. Why should I interfere? I need only two things: coal production and peaceful workers. Once you've ensured these you can do whatever you like, within the limits of the law. But let me tell you for your own good that Dhruba Khatua's a dangerous man. Don't think he owes his power to the minister alone; he's also powerful in his own right. What's more, Harishankar Patnaik is weak. You can't depend on him if you want to run the show here. That aside, he's not going to cause you any trouble. If you can run your unit with his aid, go ahead and do that. I haven't any objections at all.'

He realized he had to give the general manager the news. He dialled the general manager's office.

'There's been a strike in the colliery, sir. Workers aren't going into the pit.'

'So I've heard.' Mr Mirchandani remained calm and unruffled.

'We could perhaps issue a notice about a week's pay cut, sir?'

'That's your call.'

'Or should I inform the police?'

'Deshmukh, earlier I said I wouldn't meddle in affairs coming under your jurisdiction. You're responsible for your own realm. I've mentioned the two things I want: production and peace. You're accountable for these. It's your job to put an end to the strike by whatever means possible. That's all. I don't want to hear any more from you. I'm hoping that the next time you call me it'll be to say the problem's been fixed. I don't want to hear anything else in between.'

Mr. Mirchandani put the receiver down. He spoke the last words harshly and with some annoyance. Deshmukh felt at a loss. What was Mr Mirchandani's true face? What did he want? In the afternoon he had seemed well under control, but just now he had exploded. Was he unhappy with Deshmukh's behaviour and actions? The way he had acted this afternoon had not given Deshmukh even the faintest hint of that.

Mr Naidu phoned him later and asked, 'What did the general manager say, sir?'

Deshmukh did not know what to say and felt very insecure, as if he had been abandoned on the battlefield with enemies closing in on him from all sides with guns, mocking him as he stood there brandishing the only weapon he had. And he could feel rising within him a desperate cry for help.

TWELVE

With the increasing body ache and muscle pain, Pradyumna knew he was coming down with a high fever. The nurse, poised to remove his stitches, felt his brow. 'You're running a temperature', she said. 'Have you seen a doctor? Your wound seems to have become infected.'

Pradyumna had never liked hospitals; their smell made him feel sick. Besides, as Samaru Khadia, a mere casual loader, he had to stand in the queue at the doctor's chambers for hours, and he did not like that. But see a doctor he must. So he had gone and, like many times in the past, the doctor had written out a prescription without examining him. 'The stitches have been in for eight days', Pradyumna had volunteered. Without so much as a word the doctor ordered the removal of the sutures.

The nurse pulled the tape off his face with a jerk, taking with it the medicated gauze bandage underneath. She bent over to look at the wound. Her face was so close to Pradyumna he was able to see the thin wisps of dark hair under her nose. 'There's pus around two of the stitches', she said.

The nurse cut the stitches and gave him a pill. 'This will bring down your temperature right away, but you need to see the doctor. He'll put you on antibiotics.'

Pradyumna caught a glimpse of his reflection in the window of the dressing room. He could not help but notice the ugly scar that had formed under his nose. He had always thought of himself as unattractive. It made him feel bad about himself. He had high cheekbones, which made him look older than his age. A thin bony body, an ageing face, and now this scar. He must look even more hideous. He felt anxious and avoided going to see the doctor. After leaving the hospital, a terrible chill descended upon him. His feet lacked the strength to move. Where would he go? To his uncle's house? To the eatery? To the betel shop? To the post office? The strike had been on for so many days now. The Dhruba Khatua gang had called the strike and thrown its weight behind it. Except for management everybody else was staying away from the pit. The atmosphere was thick with tension. Pradyumna had the distinct impression people were avoiding him. Because he was a member of the new union's executive body, the members of the old union kept their distance. Not even ordinary workers seemed to be on easy terms with him.

So where would Pradyumna go? Despite having stayed with his uncle's family for a long time, he did not feel at home there. He lived like a guest, unable to freely move about the house or to crash onto the bed or call for food when he was hungry. The best he could do when he went home was silently sit on a tin chair.

What he needed at this moment were a cot and a blanket to fend off the chilling circle of fever engulfing him. He wanted to lose himself under a blanket. He wanted to forget himself, to give no answers to anyone for a few moments. But he did not have a home. This rendered him even more helpless, bringing to his mind his village home, his father and mother and elder sisters. Pradyumna felt miserable.

He found himself in front of a food stall without knowing how he had gotten there. He sat on a bench and leaned against a wooden pole. His breath felt warm. The part of his face from where his stitches had been removed was throbbing. From childhood he had been weak. His mother used to say he was not able to put up with the slightest of pain. But now, he had been able to put up with everything, the stitches on his face and the fever. Had he ever imagined leaving his home and village, coming so far away, and living a solitary life? In his village, he had been afraid to sleep in a room alone. Now he did that. Ever since he was small, he had tossed and turned while sleeping, changing from one side to another, but sleep would elude him. Everyone at home resented his fidgeting as he slept. But in Uncle Agani's house he kept still, afraid the sound of the bed creaking would disturb his uncle or aunt's sleep. How had he been able to change so much? Would he be able to accept these changes and spend the rest of his days as Samaru Khadia?

He called for the boy at the eatery and ordered a glass of water and some tea. He washed down the pill for the fever with the water. He was just about to lift the glass of tea to his mouth when he heard someone addressing him. The voice was loud. Despite his pain, he turned his head to see who had spoken. A worker sitting next to him had just greeted him. The man was drunk; his breath smelled of country liquor. Earlier, he had not been as familiar with that smell, but at the colliery liquor was so common his fear and agitation about it was ebbing away. The man had drunk too much and was greeting Pradyumna too loudly. He knew by now that drunkards tended to speak loudly without realizing it.

In the village, Pradyumna had never felt at ease while conversing with friends. He always had the feeling no one paid any attention to him because of some flaw in his personality. The boys working in tea stalls at the bus stop in his village or in Sakhigopal or even in Puri seemed to ignore him. But then here in the colliery he had been able to recover his true self. Paradoxical, since it was here he had lost his identity! Perhaps that is how it worked: you gain something after you lose something. Everyone here knew he was not Samaru Khadia, knew that he was a Brahmin boy. It was as though the name Samaru Khadia was a mask. Everybody realized that he was playacting, wearing a mask, and that the man underneath was a different person altogether. But why should Pradyumna take such things to heart? Why should he feel he had lost his identity?

'This strike is a trick of that bloody Deshmukh sahib', said the man. 'What do you say to that? I know Dhruba Khatua inside out: he's a bloody stooge of management.'

Pradyumna was caught unawares. It was not good to say such things at the eatery. If somebody from Khatua's gang was around, they would surely create a scene. Pradyumna hurriedly finished his tea and got up. He put his hand on the man's shoulder, saying, 'We'll talk about this later. It's getting late. I'm going.'

Then he left. He had learnt to be clever. He was no longer a simple village lad who had not seen anything of the world. Would he have been able to escape the drunkard in Puri or Sakhigopal? Perhaps not. Pradyumna had become worldly wise after coming to the colliery, not one to be fooled by sweet and sleek talk. People often portrayed themselves as simple and straightforward, but he knew that in reality they were shrewd and selfish. Take this man who had shown such concern even though he was inebriated. If he had such distaste for Dhruba Khatua, or if Harishankar Patnaik was his beloved leader, then why wasn't he ending his strike and going back to work? Pradyumna knew everyone through and through. Not a single bloody one was any good!

Pradyumna left the eatery and started to walk down the road. He felt as if the colliery, the colony, and the dirty and disorganised people around him did not exist, as if by moving away from them he was sinking back into his circle of fever. The air from his nostrils was warm; his eyes were welling up, as if tears might fall at any moment. He found it difficult to raise his head. He was tottering.

He headed towards his uncle's house. His small, skull-like room under an asbestos roof was his only refuge. The other people he shared the house with seemed to be aliens from another planet; in their midst he could never be himself. Yet these people were part of his milieu, of his present existence. It was they who constituted the entire universe of Samaru Khadia.

By the time Pradyumna reached his uncle's house he was unable to raise his head. How he wished someone would give him a bed to sleep on! Wrapped up in a blanket he would have let his imagination carry him away. Maybe to the portals of a huge hall or to a sea beach, or to the rooftop of the Duduwala Dharmasala, or maybe even to Minakshi's lap. With his eyes closed, he would have flown into space with the help of the wings he had suddenly grown. Or he would have sunk into the watery depths and dug from the mud the tiny container in which lay locked the secret of the old ogress's death. He would have listened, half asleep, to his father reciting the Bhagabata and to snatches of his sisters' conversation rising above the sound of the television serial. He would have felt the soft touch of his mother's hand on his back, as she uttered the sweet words, 'Get up my dear, get up, and eat something.'

Harishankar Babu had come to speak to Uncle Agani. Both were serious and quiet. Inside the house, his aunt was hitting Sonu and he was crying piteously. This was probably a way for his aunt to express her resentment at Harishankar Babu's presence. Pradyumna glanced in the direction of the bedroom. He could see Runu and Jhunu lying on the bed, quiet, with their eyes fixed on the ceiling.

'Has your wound healed, Pradyumna?' Harishankar asked.

Pradyumna did not want to talk. Maybe he should have told them what the nurse at the hospital had said about the wound, placing emphasis on the wound, the two stitches that had become infected, and his fever. But he did not; in fact, he could not. This was who he was, never forthcoming. He should have perhaps been more like the others. Then he could really have become Pradyumna instead of Samaru Khadia.

'The strike led by Dhruba Khatua and his group has been going on for three days', said Harishankar. 'This is a challenge to our union. Somehow, we have to keep the mine running. This is a time to fight. And Pradyumna, we have to win this battle. We've decided we'll force our way down into the mine today. You'll be in the first group to go down.'

'Me?' This came as a surprise to Pradyumna. He had a fever and should have mentioned that before. If he did now, these people would think he was simply pretending because he was afraid. Still he ventured, 'I have a fever. Two of my stitches have turned septic.'

His uncle replied with a hint of annoyance in his voice, 'Aah! Stop pretending. Do you think you're going down to work? You'll simply have to show your face and get your name entered in the register.'

Pradyumna was on the verge of tears. He was really in pain, in real pain. Couldn't he convince anyone of his illness, his helplessness? Or were the others so preoccupied with their own affairs they did not have time to spare a thought for him? But Pradyumna was unable to say anything. Why had he really joined the union? He himself did not know. He knew unions sacrificed problems of the individual in the interest of those of the larger group. The sacrifice of one for the sake of the many was glorified. But weren't the many also pressed into service for the benefit of just one? Weren't the masses often used for what the leaders wanted? How justified had Pradyumna been in thinking he was separate from the group when, just a little while ago, he had thought people, caught up in their own worlds, were not able to share in his sorrow and suffering? Wasn't Pradyumna cutting himself off from the group and becoming trapped in his own small world? His head started to reel. Perhaps it was not good to brood so much. Perhaps the world and life were not so complex after all. The habit of looking at things from different perspectives made them into such a tangled ball of thread.

Uncle Agani asked Pradyumna to come with him to the hospital. 'I'll get the doctor to declare you fit', he said.

The strike at Tarbahar Colliery had entered its third day, but there was no mention of it in the newspaper or on the regional news round up on the radio or on the national news channel, Doordarshan. When he thought about all this, Pradyumna felt despondent. In what godforsaken place had he ended up? Separated from the world, in exile, and drifting aimlessly. How small and negligible was this Tarbahar Colliery in the context of the world, of India, and even of Odisha! Here was Pradyumna Mishra, existing in this place anonymously and without any purpose. And how small and insignificant his anguish for others was! He even doubted whether Harishankar Babu and his uncle understood his mental agony. It was as if he was a toy gun for them, ready to go off at the pull of a trigger. It was as if he had no say in the matter, no personal opinion, no personal likes or dislikes.

When Pradyumna went to the pit, he felt better; his aches and pains had largely disappeared. The fever was probably gone, but he was feeling very weak, as if he might dissolve. He had not gone to work for fifteen to twenty days, and now was afraid to go down into the pit. He felt the same fear that had overwhelmed him when he had gone down for the first time. His knees got stiff, from going down and coming up just once. He had difficulty making the trek from the pithead to Uncle Agani's house. In the early days, Pradyumna would slip into a deep sleep when he returned from work, but even after sleeping for eight to nine hours at a stretch his eyes would still be sleep-filled. His aunt resented his sleeping like a corpse during the daytime and was constantly making pointed remarks. Pradyumna was unable to wake up, though he knew he was the cause of her tantrums. He kept lying in bed, pretending to be asleep. Later on, of course, he got used to the work and no longer felt as overcome by fatigue. As he went to the pithead today, he remembered those early days and began to feel listless again. He felt he would not have the strength to come back up to the surface once he had gone down into the depths. Or maybe if he did somehow get out, he would lack the energy to walk from the pithead to his uncle's house.

The clerks sat in the office of the timekeepers. The lamp cabin was deserted. Usually full of people, it was eerily empty today. The only sounds came from the charging batteries and the conveyor belt. The coal-loaded trucks were not running. Helmets, baskets, shovels, black belts for the batteries and lamps all remained in their places. Only three to four workers, including Pradyumna, led by his uncle, were standing before the timekeepers' office. Piling up the lamps he brought from the lamp cabin, a clerk said, 'What are these three or four workers going to do? Where are the loaders? We need to raise coal, do you see? We need output.'

These questions vexed Uncle Agani. 'They're going to work in name only', he replied.

Pradyumna thought Dhruba Khatua's followers would be picketing near the pithead and stopping workers from going down into the mine. He had come prepared for the worst, but when he arrived there was nothing, no picketing or slogans on the walls and fences. His uncle remarked, 'It was a mistake for management to issue a seven-day pay-cut notice. Those who missed a day's work thought it best not to come in because they would be facing a week's pay-cut anyway. They'll show up on the eighth day.'

Once his uncle got their names logged in, he left to see if he could find any more workers. All this seemed childish to Pradyumna. But he knew how such events could be idealized and how meaning could be ascribed to these small childish things. In reality, they were trivial and meaningless. Were all philosophical positions in fact equally insubstantial?

If so, then what about our life, our present time, and the sphere in which we exist? Did these go beyond prevailing beliefs and conceptions? Were they independent of what is known, learned, spoken, and expressed?

Pradyumna felt very confused; it was dizzying to think about all this. It was like trying to find the end of a ball of yarn. He did not know where it began, where it went, where the knot was tied, and where it was fastened. He was never able to reach a firm and clear decision, never able to regard anything as a guiding truth. He tended to doubt everything. Each step he took seemed hesitant, weak, and apprehensive. Every sentence he uttered was coloured by timidity and diffidence.

Pradyumna entered the number of the lamp in the register the clerk was holding up and let the battery dangle from the holder attached to his waist. He fixed the lamp to his helmet. One among them asked, 'Shall we go down?'

The clerk sat with his face buried in the register. 'The canteen's closed. No one's shown up.'

'What will we do once we're down there? The loader seems to be absent.'

The clerk, who was bent over writing in the register, raised his head, and stared at them angrily. 'Why are you asking me? Go ask your manager. Go ask your foreman. Go ask that leader of yours who brought you here.'

Pradyumna walked away. He paced back and forth for a while in the lamp cabin and read the numbers of the lamps on the charger. He went near the manager's office and saw some members of the staff were engaged in a game of cards.

He did not know what duty had been assigned to him. He was a casual loader. Earlier, he had worked as a tub checker. So he should now be assigned loading work. Would he have to load tubs today?

'Let me see your face. Is this where you were hit? Ah, what a bad cut! How many stitches? Looks like it'll leave a permanent scar.'

Pradyumna turned around and saw that the person patting him on his back was a mining sardar. He could not remember whether the man went by the name of Mishra or Panda or Nayak or Das. He had certainly seen the man many times, but had never spoken with him before.

The mining sardar said, 'Come, let's go down. One trip and our work's done.'

Pradyumna started to walk behind the mining sardar without saying a word. The path leading down into the mine felt a lot like going down into a cave. A big hole with steps. A picture of the goddess Kali had been hung at the mouth of the pit, a time-honoured practice in a coal mine. Everyone bowed to the picture before going down. At first, Pradyumna was afraid. His legs had trembled the day he had first descended. He was scared the roof would cave in or the trolleys moving in the dark would run into him. That day, he had caught a glimpse of death, of its terror, and realized how much he loved life. Over time, all these sensations lost their sharp edges. Now, the world below seemed very much like the world above. These days, nothing was ever out of the ordinary anywhere for Pradyumna.

Yet today fear grabbed hold of Pradyumna as he climbed down the ladder in that cave-like place. Everything was pitch dark. The light from the lamp on his helmet seemed feeble in the face of the darkness. The area underground was huge, but there was no one in sight. Pradyumna's hair stood on end.

'I never got a chance to talk to you before', said the mining sardar, who was leading the way. 'You've turned into quite a hero. Everyone in the colliery, from officer to loader, knows who you are.'

The words echoed back at them. Pradyumna had never heard an echo when people were at work down below.

'Why did a boy like you join the union?' asked the mining sardar. 'The union's for power brokers. To tell the truth, the union's been tarnished by political leaders. Think about how things have changed of late, how the leftist ideology of Russia and China is disappearing. I feel sad when I think about an ideology being lost. I'm not a communist, but the death of communism saddens me.'

Pradyumna was no communist and had not given much thought to communism. He did have a smattering of knowledge about Marxism, Perestroika, the Gang of Four, Stalin, Bakunin, the Cultural Revolution, etc., but he had never bothered much about these. The decline of communism had not particularly affected him.

'You might want to believe trade unionism goes along with Marxism or the dictatorship of the proletariat, but for me these two things are incompatible. Do you know what 'incompatible' means?'

Pradyumna shook his head. What level of education must this mining sardar have? He must not have graduated from mining school. If he had, he would have become a foreman. He must have been enrolled as a casual loader and inched his way upwards, sitting first for the gas-testing examination, and then for the first-aid test. Finally, he would have passed the certificate course for mining sardar. How had he picked up so many things? For Pradyumna the colliery was a den of dunces. There were many technically qualified people here, with diplomas and degrees, but no one seemed to have real intelligence. Whether officer or staff, no one knew about anything other than about the coal mine—turnover, output, and breakdown—or about partying, gambling, and drinking.

'Incompatible'—how can I explain that to you? Well, take the moon and the sun, they're incompatible with each other, since they never exist together at the same time. Likewise, trade unionism has nothing to do with Marxism. A trade union always takes the middle path. It tries to provide workers with common pleasures and privileges in the name of protecting them from exploitation. As a result, workers get used to having others provide for them. All that sloganeering about fighting and protesting against exploitation is only meant to delude people. Trade unions never want to alienate themselves from management. On the contrary, they help to contain the resentment of the workers against management. Have you ever thought about this?'

Darkness reigned everywhere. A twenty-watt neon light was flickering in the distance. The light from the lamp on the helmet was too weak to show the face of the mining sardar in front of him. Everything seemed eerie to Pradyumna. Did this man really belong to the colliery? Or was all this unreal? Was he hallucinating? Could this be happening?

'Come, let's go to the upper storey. There's nothing to do except check things out.' The mining sardar turned around and took Pradyumna by the hand. 'Your body's blistering hot. Why did you choose to climb down with such a high fever? Okay, sit here. Sit down and wait for me while I take a look upstairs.'

The mining sardar left him there and climbed up the stairs. Pradyumna sat in the huge mine, in utter darkness. Was he starting to dream? It was dark all around. A spooky sound floated in from a distance. He had not heard it when the mining sardar was with him, but now the sound was loud and clear. At first, he was startled, but then he remembered that the fan-house outlet pipe was somewhere nearby. The fan house expelled air from inside the mine. Back in his village, Pradyumna had earned a bad name for being easily scared. He was afraid of the dark; he was not willing to sleep alone in a room. But then he was all alone here underground. Was the person who had gone upstairs a human being? Would he be able to hear Pradyumna if he screamed? Or was he a ghost who had tricked him into coming here?

Pradyumna had never questioned the existence of ghosts and spirits. He had not given much thought to many other things in this world and had no opinion about them. But he was afraid of the dark. It felt as if someone was circling around him. At times some hideous-looking person seemed to be staring at him from the darkness, frightening him. Was it a ghost, or simply a figment of his imagination?

There was darkness everywhere, a kind of darkness that could be called prehistoric. Many years ago, many millions of years ago, this place must have been inhabited by primeval forms of life. Today, after so many eons, Pradyumna and these forms were coming face to face. He felt as if a shape was issuing out of the wall, out of the darkness, out of the encrustations of coal, laughing a devilish laugh.

Pradyumna's hands and limbs began to shiver. Is there ever any real basis for fear? After all, fear is still fear, whether there is an actual basis for it or not, and no matter how clearly things are explained. He felt a vein near his ear stretching. He felt like dancing a macabre dance. He wanted to frighten someone, make a hideous face baring his teeth with his eyes bulging. He wanted to pass off as a ghost, an apparition. He was not Pradyumna. No, not Samaru Khadia either. He was another force. He would go on a rampage; he would kill and devour. He would blow to bits those who were out to erase his existence; he would suck their blood and bone marrow, chew their flesh, and tear them to shreds, reducing them to nothing.

Pradyumna let out a blood-curdling yell. He leapt on to the battlefield with a triumphant war cry. His eyes, nose, and ears looked unnatural and fierce. Was he sprouting claws and fangs? Had he turned into Narasimha, that fearsome deity, who was part man and part lion? Was he a demon?

Pradyumna's body was shaking. He found it difficult to breathe. Darkness was gradually closing in on him.

*

When he came to, Pradyumna discovered he was lying on a surface. Two or three people were sitting around, leaning over him. His ears were sore, as though water had been spilled into them. When he tried to get up to sit, the mining sardar forced him down on his back. 'Lie down. There's nothing to be afraid of. You lost consciousness inside the pit.'

'Are you sick? Have you fainted before?'

'Why did you go down into the mine with such a high fever?'

'Why are you crowding around? Make room for the air to circulate.'

Pradyumna shrank within himself. How had he fainted in the presence of so many people? He only wanted to get up and flee. Was he still running a fever? 'I want to be on my way', he said. 'I feel a little better.'

'Have you seen a doctor about your fever? Would you like to go to a hospital?'

Pradyumna got up off the floor and sat on a chair. Quite a large crowd had gathered around him. Most of the people were mining staff or timekeepers or under managers. Beyond the people around him, he could see the sky above the pithead. Evening had descended. The lights were on in all the offices. What time could it be?

He caught the drift of the conversation buzzing around
him: the strike had been called off. There had been a truce
between Dhruba Khatua and Deshmukh. Work would
resume from the night shift today.

'Is the strike really over?' Did Pradyumna ask someone
this? Did he have anyone in mind? No one said a word by
way of an answer.

THIRTEEN

Was defeat now certain for Harishankar? Is that how defeat steals in? Imperceptibly, as ordinary as the sky, the earth, the sun, the moon, the wind and storms, falling leaves, blossoming flowers, radios playing songs, little boys running about? Like an ordinary person, shaking your hand and asking how you are. It had crept up on Harishankar while he was sleeping and sat on a corner of his cot. Harishankar had shifted his legs to make room for it. It had made little coughing noises and wiped away the beads of perspiration on Harishankar's face with the end of its dhoti. It had looked at him as if it needed a glass of water and would have been obliged to be given one.

When the news of his defeat reached Harishankar, he was lying on his string cot reading the newspaper. In fact, he was not reading; he was only holding the paper open in front of him. His mind was filled with thoughts of the strike, Dhruba Khatua, the workers and employees of Tarbahar Colliery, the general manager, and Mr Deskmukh. At that very moment Agani arrived on his bicycle. With one foot on the pedal and the other on the ground, he asked, with

a touch of sarcasm in his voice, 'Are you up on the latest
news, Netaji? Deshmukh and Dhruba Khatua reached an
agreement at a secret meeting. I got fifteen workers from
the second shift to go down into the pit. If that bloody
Deshmukh sahib had held out for two more days, the strike
would have been broken.'

Had Dhruba Khatua won and called off the strike?
Harishankar had been unable to break it. His defeat could
not have more crushing!

Harishankar could not blame Deshmukh; he had given
enough time. Three days. That should have been enough
for Harishankar to show what he could do.

Now Harishankar had most certainly been sidelined.
Discarded. He had proved he was out of touch. Good
for nothing. Should he have jumped back into union
politics like this? Or perhaps Deshmukh did not count for
much and never had. Maybe Dhruba Khatua too was not
important. Hema Babu was the force behind Dhruba's
win, and perhaps even Hema Babu himself did not matter;
the power he had as a minister counted for everything.
From the very start, Harishankar had understood how far
power could reach and how much of an impact it could
have. Many had pushed him to act against Hema Babu,
to leave his group and join another. But Harishankar had
not been able to do that. If he had not been encouraged
by the general manager, Mr Mirchandani, to start
another union, he would never have gotten around to
confronting Dhruba Khatua. But, then, he could not
blame Mr Mirchandani either. The man had given him

enough support. Perhaps it was Harishankar who did not have any power or influence.

Had Harishankar known he would not be able to form a union unless he had the support of management? Yes. Could any union in this democratic nation exist without management's support? Did it have to be like that? Should it be? How could a trade union, formed to protect the interests of workers, avoid its responsibility and fall back upon management? Wasn't that a huge betrayal?

When Harishankar was still young and had first entered trade union politics, Hema Babu had not been overly ambitious. For Harishankar, management was a class enemy. How had everything changed? How had that dream, that hope, and that passion faded? Well, Harishankar himself had accepted the blessings of management. Perhaps his aspirations had not been very high, perhaps he had never tried to use the union for personal gain, but if that was the case why was it that he had wanted to set up a union? Was he so completely devoid of self-interest? Had it really never occurred to him to use the union to assert his own power and authority? Had he truly wanted the union to prevent the workers from being exploited? And even if he had, had he ever taken steps to make that happen?

'Netaji, if we're to survive this, we have to adopt new tactics', said Agani. 'Or else management won't give a damn about us. Dhruba Khatua will start maligning us. The workers won't trust us. Now that this is where we've ended up, we have to continue to fight. Should we call a meeting of the executive body to discuss this?'

Harishankar sat up. He folded the newspaper. 'Do as you like, Agani. I'm at my wits' end.'

Agani got off his bicycle and put it on its stand. He took out his handkerchief and wiped his face. Sitting down on the cot next to Harishankar, he continued. 'Look Netaji, our union's only a baby at the moment. Its most basic needs haven't yet been met. A formal membership drive hasn't been launched. The union's starved for funds. There's not even a place that can serve as an office. It will only achieve some stability once it has overcome its teething problems. The big issue for us now is not to figure out why Deshmukh sahib secretly agreed with Dhruba Khatua to break the strike he himself had engineered. What will cause us a great deal of trouble in the future is the deal itself between the two. The news I have about it is that the terms of the deal allow the company to consult only with Dhruba Khatua's union on policy matters and deny our union the right to sign up members. If these decisions are implemented, then our union would be strangled. I think we should call a meeting of our executive body today. But before doing that, it would be a good idea to talk to Deshmukh sahib.'

'What have you decided to do?' asked Harishankar, wanting to know about the future course of action.

'I have thought of something. How about a hunger strike?'

'A hunger strike? These days they're a farce.'

When Hema Babu was in charge of the union Harishankar had staged many such dramatic hunger strikes, many of them at the leader's request. They had never accomplished anything. Harishankar had organized such fake displays, with people eating cold and stale vadas and pakoras under the darkness of night and of going back on strike after emptying their bowels outside. The end of the strikes had been decided before they even started. Who would drink fruit juice, and when, what would be announced, who would take part in the procession, and what their slogans would be—the entire programme would be drawn up beforehand. Gandhi had used fasting as a weapon, but these days it had become merely a clever trick to influence people and to gain publicity. A farce really.

'A farce? You call going on a hunger strike a farce?'Agani asked.

Harishankar became irritated. 'You've got experience, Agani; you've been involved in union affairs for a long time. Besides, I consider you a practical man. Do you seriously believe hunger strikes accomplish anything these days? Don't you know hunger strikes are nothing but hoaxes?'

Agani eyed Harishankar. 'I am indeed a practical man, Netaji, and I do understand what works. But try and understand we have no other option apart from a hunger strike. I agree that such strikes don't have the importance they once had, but it's also true that if the morale is high we can achieve a lot through such actions. Do you believe that if we seriously go on a hunger strike our goals can't be achieved? Think about Punjab and Andhra Pradesh. What other than hunger strikes led to those states being formed? Look at history. It's said it repeats itself. So why not go on a hunger strike, even if you consider it a farce or a hoax, to give a new lease on life to our union?'

How had Agani become so well informed? Harishankar was surprised. He had taken Agani to be a small-time leader, but he certainly had good judgement and heightened awareness. Harishankar felt overwhelmed.

'Let's go and have a talk with Deshmukh sahib before doing anything', said Agani. 'If we have his support, we may not have to go that far.'

Harishankar felt exhausted and had no desire to get up. But Agani was in no mind to give up. 'Let's get going, Netaji.'

Harishankar had to get up. And he did so, yawning. He shook off his lethargy and slipped his feet into his slippers. 'Where shall we go?' he asked. 'What will we gain by talking to Deshmukh sahib?'

Agani did not answer. He moved forward, pushing his bicycle. Harishankar followed behind.

Stopping in front of Deshmukh's office, Agani asked the guard, 'Is sahib in?'

The guard, who was making entries in a register, remained seated. 'Write your name in the register', he answered.

Never before in Tarbahar Colliery had it been required that people enter their name in a register before going into the office. Perhaps this had been recently introduced by Deshmukh sahib. Agani wrote their names. When the guard saw what had been entered as 'purpose of visit', he said, 'Sahib's busy in an urgent meeting. He'll be seeing you later.'

'Who's inside?'

The guard was a little uneasy. 'People from the union', he said.

'Dhruba Khatua?'

'Yes.' The guard nodded his head.

Dhruba Khatua? Hearing that name was for Harishankar like receiving a slap on his face. This was not unusual at all. There was no reason why Deshmukh sahib should not meet with Dhruba Khatua. Yet Dhruba Khatua was inside, busy in an urgent meeting with Deshmukh, and Harishankar was outside—that in itself was deeply galling.

'Why not speak to sahib on the phone and tell him we've come to see him?' suggested Agani.

'I can't do that, sir. Sahib himself has said not to let anyone in.'

'Why not phone him? We'd like to hear what Deshmukh sahib says.'

The guard eyed Agani. The determined look on Agani's face gave Harishankar courage. The guard lifted the receiver and spoke, 'Sir, Harishankar Babu and Agani Hota are here to see you.' He kept the receiver close to his ear for some time and then placed it back on the cradle. With some annoyance in his voice, he asked, 'Did you hear how sahib flared up for no reason? You people have unnecessarily subjected me to a scolding.'

This was humiliating for Harishankar, especially with the guard present. Agani smiled, but the smile of the slighted. They went inside and sat on the sofa. Harishankar felt his blood rush to his ears. Was it really worth inviting an insult over such a small thing? He needed to be practical.

Harishankar felt that his time was running out, that he was quickly growing old. It was now well-nigh impossible for him to change, and a fresh start was just as impossible. He had lost the youthful passion needed to form a different type of union.

Why had Harishankar set out on a new enterprise when he was past his prime? He should have started something like this when he had first entered colliery service.

It was very hot inside the building, with its asbestos roof. Harishankar could not reach into the side pocket of his kurta for his handkerchief, and so he wiped away his perspiration with the end of his dhoti. There was a new jeep parked in the driveway in front of the building, and two or three bicycles were on their stands. Tarbahar Colliery was slowly changing. A move to computerize the offices was afoot. The dirty stain characterizing the faces of collieries was slowly being wiped away. Everything was changing.

The stark face of misery Harishankar had seen when he first came to the coal mine had all but disappeared. These days, even loaders were drawing three thousand rupees as salary. Compared to them, clerks or category-one miscellaneous labourers earning the basic wage seemed more oppressed and financially insecure.

'Netaji, we've got to meet Deshmukh somehow before we leave', said Agani. 'Didn't I tell you we'd be pushed aside? Now, Deshmukh has started to ignore us. We have to be tough, Netaji. If we go soft now, these people will simply dump us. We have to stand firm in order to survive.'

How does one fight? How do the words of a fiery speech translate into a fight, war, and conflict? Harishankar was quite unable to feel combative. He was certainly tense. In such a mental state, can one jump into battle? Maybe Harishankar had lost the ability to feel. Detached and devoid of feeling, he was only following Agani's lead.

Suddenly Dhruba Khatua and his friends barged out, pushing the office door open. Seeing Agani and Harishankar, Dhruba stopped in his tracks. A mischievous glint filled his eyes. Giving the man standing near him a shove, he commented, 'You idiot, you've become quite a leader, haven't you? You dared to call a strike?'

One of the men from the gang answered Dhruba Khatua's sarcasm, while looking at Harishankar, 'I'm a bloody stooge of management through and through. My job is to suck up to management in secret and claim all the while to have sympathy for the workers.'

'Sympathy, my foot? The bastard can't count on the support of even one worker, and yet he claims he has the sympathy of the workers', said another.

Harishankar felt his fists tighten, but no, he had to suppress his anger. Things can get out of hand if small things are allowed to get on one's nerves. But Agani flew into a rage. He turned around and looked Dhruba Khatua in the eye. 'If you dare, speak to our faces', he yelled. 'Why do you act like a village woman and speak to the walls and fences?'

Unprepared for such an attack, Dhruba Khatua was caught off guard. One person from his group came forward and shouted, 'You bloody traitor, first make sure you're strong enough and then come on out for a fight.'

Agani ran over to the man and caught him by the collar. 'What the hell!' shouted Agani. 'Who do you think you are, you son of a whore, you son-of-a-bitch? Do you think you'll be able to use the same hooliganism and beat up everyone the way you did Pradyumna and Om Prakash, because they were weak. Try to figure out how strong you really are and what is the strength of those with whom you pick a fight.' The man was not expecting such a sudden and bold attack. Holding him by the collar, Agani dragged him and shoved him into the wall. When the man slid to the floor, holding his head, Agani gave him two good kicks in the back.

All of this happened too quickly for Harishankar. What should he do? Try to pull Agani away? Prepare to face anyone from Dhruba Khatua's group who tried to counterattack? Manage the rally for Agani? In the end, he did nothing; he couldn't think of anything to do. It was as if he no longer existed in this world, as if what he had just witnessed were scenes from a film or on television, with no connection to him and beyond his control.

Hearing the commotion people ran towards the office. The security guards restrained Agani. The man who had been beaten sat on the floor in silence, his head hung low. Two or three of Dhruba Khatua's men who tried to attack Agani and overpower him were being restrained by three or four security guards. The guard keeping the register near the gate was telling the assembled crowd to disperse or take their fight outside if they were so keen on it. In the same breath, he was yelling for a certain Ramdhan to go and inform the police and was appealing to Dhruba Khatua and Agani to stop their brawl. At one point he approached Harishankar. 'Did you see that, Netaji?' he asked. 'I'll get a good hiding from sahib today for sure. Why did you people have to stay?'

Both by force and through coaxing, the security guards led Dhruba's group outside the office building. They knew nothing new would come out of these fights, and so they left, after yelling at Agani and Harishankar and calling them names.

Agani was still as angry as ever. For long he had been on the sidelines, and did not want to miss out on the chance to act like a hero in front of the gathered crowd. He did not seek permission before letting loose a tirade against the guard and Deshmukh sahib. Then he took Harishankar by the hand and dragged him into the office, pushing open the door to the waiting room. The corridor was buzzing with people. Everyone was waiting, eager to learn what would happen. Agani only stopped when both he and Harishankar were inside Deshmukh sahib's room. This time the guard outside the room lacked the courage to block their entry. Or maybe Agani barged in before the guard could think of stopping him. When the door opened Deshmukh sahib was seated behind a desk across from them. Agani and Harishankar did not know what to do. The handle of the door slipped from their grasp, and the door slammed shut. Deshmukh sahib smiled calmly as if nothing had happened, as if he was totally unaware of the brawl outside. With a smile he said, 'Good morning! Please come in. Take a seat.'

The air cooler was whirring almost inaudibly in the room. An expensive cooler. The fragrance of an air freshener filled the room. They could feel the softness of the carpet under their feet. Costly distemper covered the wall. A bookshelf filled with files and books stood near the desk, and various sorts of graphs were hung on the wall. Harishankar and Agani sat down. Deshmukh sahib smiled, the smile of a victor. The peon came and placed two cups of tea on the desk without waiting to be asked. Harishankar suddenly did not know why he had come. Didn't he have something important to tell Deshmukh sahib? What exactly? The cool and soothing air in the room made him feel drowsy. With great effort he suppressed his yawn, and before Deshmukh could say anything he lifted the cup of tea to his lips.

Agani opened the conversation. 'You were trying to avoid us, sir?'

'Avoid you?' Was Deshmukh sahib merely pretending to be surprised? 'You people are dear to me', he answered. 'Why would I avoid you?'

'But you scolded the guard over phone a little while ago.'

'Scolded him? Perhaps the guard was lying. Should I call and ask him?'

'Look sir. There's no need to interrogate or intimidate him. From the way you spoke on the phone we understood perfectly well you were scolding him.'

Agani was just an ordinary worker; where did such self-confidence come from? How was he able to sit in front an E-4 or E-5 executive and argue with him? Harishankar would have miserably failed at that. Because of this inability he had never amounted to much. Would it have been appropriate if he had sat with his chest puffed out and his head raised? But instead he sat bent over, his head hanging low, his back bent. He tried to sit up straight like Agani. He rested on his elbows and looked at Deshmukh.

Deshmukh looked Agani in the eye and spoke in a serious tone. 'A meeting with the union members was going on.'

'Union? Which union, may I ask? Dhruba Khatua's, wasn't it?'

'Well, yes; for the time being that's the only recognized union.'

'Is that written in stone? A union that hasn't held elections for the past three years, a union that didn't register a single person last month, a union that doesn't enjoy the backing of the people—is that what you consider a recognized union?' Agani asked, clearing his throat and sitting upright.

'Well', answered Deshmukh sahib. 'It's not our job to check if a union has registered new members, or, if it has, how many. As for having the support of the people—during the recent strike it was crystal clear who commanded their support and who did not. I gave you people three days. Were you able to break the strike?'

Agani felt slightly ill at ease, but he soon regained control of himself. 'Is that enough to prove their group enjoys popular support?' he retorted. 'They stopped the workers, using goons and force. Do you want us to do the same? Do you want us to demonstrate our power by calling another strike?'

Deshmukh became irritated. 'Why can't you people understand? We won't show you any respect until you've proven how strong you are.'

'But the agreement you've made with Dhruba Khatua puts our very existence at risk. You haven't permitted us to sign up members nor are you prepared to have discussions with our union. Tell us how we can survive?'

Deshmukh sahib broke into a smile. 'That's the point. You people aren't ready to form a union; you need our support to survive. Do you think we'll keep you alive only so you can cut our throats? Well, remember this. You'll get to our necks only on your own. And, by the by, what's your name? Which pit are you assigned to? What's the incline number?'

Agani seemed a little crestfallen, but did not stop himself from hitting back at Deshmukh sahib. 'Look, we know what we're up to. We know what stand to take and when. The day we rise up, your corrupt regime will collapse. Who do you think you are? Lord Indra or the Moon God? We are union members. We are sons of this soil and will remain on this soil. Sahibs like you will come in droves but flee if we so much as lift a finger.'

Deshmukh's face hardened. He looked at Harishankar. 'Patnaik Babu, I may be on friendly terms with you, but that doesn't mean I'll suffer any uncouth person coming into my office with you and taking a chair.'

'I am not uncouth, Mr Deshmukh', shouted Agani. 'I am the president of our union. I have every right to sit here in front of you and speak.'

'The importance of your union can be judged by the fact someone like you calls himself the president. Which union is it?'

Agani stood up, trembling with rage. 'Do you want to see which union it is? Do you really care? Alright. In this coal mine, it's either you or our union. Very soon that will be decided.'

Agani stormed out of the office. Harishankar continued to sit there in silence, face to face with a grave looking Deshmukh. He was ill at ease. He had to apologize to Deshmukh sahib, but could not decide if he should apologize for Agani or argue on his behalf?

Harishankar sat there quietly. Silence filled the room. The air cooler had stopped working; it wasn't making a sound. The ticking of a clock could be heard.

Deshmukh was sombre and silent. Harishankar sat with his head down. What should he do? Get up and leave without a word? Say something as he left? Where had Agani gone? Would he be waiting outside? Would Agani feel hurt because Harishankar had stayed in the room and had not left with him? Would he think Harishankar was trying to please Deshmukh? Why hadn't he left? Did he not dare to rebel against Deshmukh? But who was Deshmukh anyway? Until yesterday he had not cared for Deshmukh? Why hadn't he got up and left?

Deshmukh sahib took out his handkerchief and wiped his forehead. 'Leave me now Patnaik Babu. I have lots to attend to. Please don't disturb me.'

These words hurt Harishankar deeply. Why had he remained seated? He could have spared himself this embarrassment. He got up and made his exit. When he got past the door he remembered that, in his haste, he had not said goodbye to Deshmukh. Would Deshmukh sahib feel bad about this?

*

In the evening, some thirty odd people gathered in front of Harishankar's house. They were all members of the new union. It was Agani who had called them there. Where would Harishankar seat so many people? His younger son went out and got three cloth mats from the neighbours. Those were not enough.

Harishankar and Agani sat on a string cot. Harishankar knew Agani's face-off with Dhruba and Deshmukh earlier in the day had spread throughout the mine. There was no newspaper here, but news, whatever it might be, circulated widely very quickly. Every wall of every house in the colony was porous. Everyone knew what went on in everyone else's house. Their sins and virtues, highs and lows were open secrets.

Harishankar knew that people in the colony would gossip to their heart's content about today's union-related fight, but that none would come forward. These thirty people who had come running to him were his resource, his weapon, his people.

Agani began by addressing them all. 'So brothers, no more formal meetings. There's very little time. We will be on a hunger strike from tomorrow. For this we need to get a tent, a mike, and cushions. We'll have to build a raised platform at the venue tonight. So before we do all that, let me know what you think. Are you willing to go on a hunger strike or not?'

The thirty people answered as one: 'We are. We are.'

Om Prakash's leg was in a cast. He had come limping, leaning on a stick, and stood in a corner. He came forward and spoke in Hindi. 'Brothers, I second what our president, Hota Babu, has proposed. People wouldn't treat monkeys or their dogs the way Deshmukh sahib has behaved with our union today. Brothers . . .'

Agani stopped him dead. 'No time for long speeches now, Om Prakash. Come, let's get our work sorted out.'

Om Prakash was not able to finish his speech. Harishankar kept sitting in silence; no one asked him what he thought. No one asked him if going on a hunger strike was the right thing to do. He sat quietly and listened to them make their preparations: where to get a large cloth mat, who should get the banner made and which shop should supply the cloth, the text for the banner, the number of cushions needed, where to place the order for the tent, who should write posters and what should be on them, where to get old newspapers for people to sit on, who should supply the ink, at whose house the glue would be prepared, where to get the microphone and the radio cassette player.

'Let's have one. Netaji can listen to the news bulletins. Some might want to listen to Bibidh Bharati', someone suggested.

'How about bringing a portable television?'

'Why not you bring your wife along?' another one said, shutting up the conversation

Harishankar did not speak a word. People were upbeat. It was as if they were getting ready for a picnic the following morning. Finally, Agani finished his list. 'Now we have to decide who will take part in the hunger strike', he said.

Om Prakash was the first to volunteer. 'I'll go on a hunger strike.'

Agani warned him. 'Keep quiet! Do you know what it means to fast until death? You're not well. Who would care for you there? Besides, the people there to assist those on strike are as useful and important as the strikers themselves. Five people will go on a fast; another five will keep them company for eight hours in a relay hunger strike; another five will keep watch for eight hours. They'll have lathis and knives, especially at night, and be there to ward off any attack by Dhruba Khatua's goons.'

Someone from the crowd spoke up. 'Hota Babu, please call out the names. We'll carry out the duties given to us. What do you think?'

The assembled men shouted, 'That's right. That's right.'

Agani stood up. 'Netaji, I suggest three people: Pradyumna, my nephew, who is employed here under the alias of Samaru Khadia; Mitrabhanu from the production section; and Chandrasekhar from the workshop. What do you think?'

The crowd shouted again. 'Yes, that's right.'

Agani asked, 'What do you have to say, Netaji? What do you think?'

What could Harishankar say? He looked up at the sky. A star or two was beginning to twinkle. Soon night would fall. And after the night, the fast unto death would begin.

FOURTEEN

Anita was seated with a belt around her neck. From it rose a rope that went around a pulley dangling from a hook in the ceiling. Then it dropped towards the floor, weighted down by the one and a half bricks, tied to the end, providing traction. Deshmukh had put Anita in traction and was looking at his watch. When the minute hand was between eight and nine he would unhook the traction.

Anita had been suffering from spondylitis for quite some time. An X-ray had been taken at the hospital, where a young, enthusiastic doctor, overflowing with devotion for his patients, the elite of the area, had examined Anita for at least an hour. His diagnosis was that the source of the pain stemmed from a cervical rib.

A cervical rib? Such technical talk went over Deshmukh's head. The doctor had tried to explain, pointing to the X-ray. 'Look here, sir. There should be only six bones, but Madam has two extra.'

This was around the same time when Deshmukh had newly taken over from Mr Mishra. His hands were full; he did not have a moment to spare. Anita was in terrible pain.

Deshmukh was not interested in knowing what 'a cervical rib' was but only wanted Anita to find some relief. If she was indisposed, his home and his world would be thrown into disarray. 'Please have her seen by a specialist, sir', the doctor had said. 'There's Dr P. Tejeswar Rao in Cuttack. He's known all over India.'

'Could I consult Dr Kulkarni? He's a renowned orthopaedist in Nagpur, with a practice in Bombay and Pune as well. He spends two days a week in each city. He's well-known throughout the state of Maharastra.'

Although the doctor did not know Dr Kulkarni, he agreed, and Deshmukh went to Nagpur with Anita. Nagpur was more convenient than either Burla or Cuttack. But it was quite difficult for him to get leave; the general manager had shown disapproval when he heard Deshmukh's request. Still, he felt he had to go to see Dr Kulkarni even though he was just taking up his new responsibilities and setting up the new office. Dr Kulkarni had been surprised on seeing the X-ray. 'Who calls that a cervical rib? Look at this.' Saying this, he showed Deshmukh the X-ray. 'I see six ribs. Your better half has spondylitis. She needs an injection and a few tablets, along with neck traction.'

Since that day, Anita had sat with the hangman's belt around her neck for fifteen minutes every day. For the first week there had been one brick; for the last two days this had increased to one and a half; in another five days it would go up to two.

The Dhruba Khatua union had called a strike after Deshmukh returned from seeing Dr Kulkarni. The strike in the mines and Anita's traction had coincided. Deshmukh was under great stress both at work, due to the strike, and at home, because of the pain Anita was in. The gums on the sides of her mouth were being pulled so tight the suffering was unbearable. The strike by Dhruba Khatua was followed by Harishankar's fast unto death. He and his supporters had been sitting under the tent in front of the general office for the past three days. Songs, speeches, and slogans were being blared over the speakers all day long.

What affected Deshmukh the most was Harishankar's fast. Dhruba Khatua's strike had not caused as much tension. Deshmukh was constantly aware of a person sitting outside, taking neither food nor drink. Harishankar's face flashed before his eyes while he was working in the office, reprimanding subordinates for their carelessness, when he went down into the pit for inspection, while he was attending an important meeting along with the general manager or sitting at a dinner he had hosted. Such a bold move by the man! Deshmukh felt hurt and humiliated. It was as if Harishankar Patnaik was hell bent on extracting his due, as if he was blackmailing Deshmukh. Yet Deshmukh could do nothing.

Deshmukh felt badly about interceding with the general manager time and again, but he had to keep him updated. Every time he went, Deshmukh felt a sense of inferiority weighing him down. He was rendered helpless by the general manager's diplomatic smile. So how could he take pride in his position? Surely he had become no better than a slave! He was a high-ranking officer of the government of India and yet had so little power. He felt as if someone was trying to muzzle him, making his own words, letters, and sentences seem alien to him. It felt as if his backbone was being eaten away by worms and degenerating into spondylitis.

Anita's spondylitis was severe. Her back pained constantly, and it was difficult for her to even raise her hand. Despite her acute distress he had taken her to a dinner hosted by the general manager, a dinner to which spouses had been invited. The general manager had organized the dinner for the Commercial Tax Officer of the region and his wife with an ulterior motive: to have the tax officer reduce the huge sums the coal mine owed to the government of Orissa in the financial review. The general manager had asked the finance manager to make arrangements for the dinner. A cash bribe was out of the question, the general manager had said, hinting that what the tax officer might want could be met in other ways. If he asked for a donation to some organization, it could be arranged through the contractors, but there should be no open talk or discussion about that. But first they needed a dinner, to test the waters. You all are experienced, he had said, so I can trust you to handle this in consultation with the deputy chief mining engineers in various units. You should also ask the officer if there are certain people he would like us to invite to the dinner. An invitation will be extended to them.

'You can see the kind of pain I'm in. I'm unable to keep still or feel comfortable for even a moment, and yet you want me to attend a dinner party being thrown for the Commercial Tax Officer?'

Anita was very conscious of her ego. How would Deshmukh explain his helplessness to her? How would he make her understand that the wife of the general manager had taken the lead in inviting the spouses of the deputy chief mining engineers to the dinner to please the tax officer and his wife? Anita's absence would not only make the wife of the general manager cross; the general manager himself, for whom this was an issue of prestige, would also take offence. How could he explain to Anita how important the blessings of the general manager were for him at this point in his life?

Normally the wife of the general manager and Anita got along well. Anita had phoned her. 'Madam, I'm suffering from acute pain due to spondylitis. Is it absolutely necessary for me to come for the dinner?'

Deshmukh could hear the voice at the other end. 'Of course, you have to come, Anita. How could I manage without you? You say you're in pain. Well, take some medication and come. There's a tablet called ibuprofen. If you take some, you won't feel the pain at all. The doctor once gave me that for my back. It's wonderful; let me see if I have some left.'

'I've taken enough medicine, madam. It's impossible for me to remain seated, even for a minute.'

Pretending she had not heard Anita, the wife of the general manager continued on. 'Tell me what you think, Anita, about the dishes on the menu for tonight. Fish cutlet, egg curry, chicken, a raita, a curry of potato and pointed gourd, fried rice, fruit salad, and custard. Should we have chapati, puri, or chole bature? Our cook at the guest house says he won't be able to make chole bature, but the wife of the finance manager says she knows a good chef. If we ask him, he'll make it.'

Anita put the phone down. Her eyes welled up, and she said: 'To hell with your job. I don't give a damn.'

Anita's eyes were filled with tears; the pain from her spondylitis was acute. The tears were washing away all the pride she took in Deshmukh's standing, her hatred for that dark room in the old and mildewy house in Jalna, her loveless marriage to Deshmukh and the repulsion she felt for him.

Deshmukh thought he would be able to raise the issue of the hunger strike at dinner with the general manager, which was why he was almost forcing Anita to go. Anita sat in the jeep with Deshmukh, dressed in a pata sari with makeup on. She was in so much pain she was not able to move her head or raise even a hand. Deshmukh drove very slowly. He appealed to her, 'Please, please Anita. Bear with it a little. Please help me.'

Anita bit her lips in anger, remorse, and pain—all of which were compounded by her sense that Deshmukh did not love her. Her eyes were awash with tears. Deshmukh remained rudely silent, although he understood what was going on. No one could understand what was coming over him. In whom could he confide? Who could he tell about his sense of insecurity? To whom could he convey the pain of being obliged to attend, a meaningless dinner, with Anita in such agony? The tax officer would wax eloquent at the dinner about inflation, politics, folk culture and art films, and the others would pretend to be under his charm, nodding in agreement. In his mind he pictured the scene that would soon unfold.

The tax officer: 'Wood's very cheap around here, isn't it? The jungle's being cut down at a rapid pace. Much of it was cleared to set up the colliery. I came out here two years ago. Where there had been thick forest earlier, now there are barren empty fields, serving as open-cast mines.'

The general manager: 'Do the trees planted by the government ever survive? I was told by our revenue department to oversee the planting, but I said no straightaway. That should be the responsibility of the forest department.'

The finance manager would then chip in, seeing his chance: 'Wood isn't cheap here, though. Wooden furniture's expensive too.'

'Expensive? No, it's cheap. Definitely cheaper than where I'm from.'

'Sir, there's a place some two hundred kilometres from here, deep inside a forest. You can't imagine how inexpensive furniture is there.'

'Two hundred kilometres away? That's very far, isn't it? You have to add in the cost of transportation.'

'That's nothing, sir. What are trucks for?'

'You people have trucks, but what about us?'

Seeing the fish about to take the bait, an enthusiastic finance manager would add: 'The trucks from our colliery usually take that road. Sir, please tell us when you want anything to be trucked in; our trucks are at your service.'

This sort of conversation meant nothing to Deshmukh. He had no role to play at the dinner. Throughout, he was troubled by the thought of Harishankar's hunger strike and Anita's spondylitis. A man was sitting in the darkness of the night; such was his boldness! He was not simply on strike, he was disturbing Deshmukh's peace of mind. What if this Harishankar fellow died? Did anyone really die under such circumstances? Deshmukh had learned they were taking their hunger strike seriously and not eating or drinking on the sly, not taking advantage of the cover of darkness. Right from the beginning of his fast Harishankar had stopped drinking water. Every day the doctor from the hospital went to take his blood pressure. It was dropping. His dehydration was increasing. The doctor had told Deshmukh, 'There's no cause for worry right now, sir, but if he keeps up the fast like this, then he's risking his life.'

Deshmukh wanted to take Anita to Nagpur once again, but only after the issue of Harishankar Babu's hunger strike had been resolved. Anita was finding it very difficult to move her head. Was Dr Kulkarni's diagnosis correct? What if the problem was not spondylitis but a cervical rib? Dr Kulkarni had said Anita's pain would go away soon after she began her medication, exercise, and traction. But no relief seemed to be in sight.

The dinner party was terribly painful for Deshmukh. For Anita too. When Deshmukh heard Anita in the room adjoining the dining hall, telling the womenfolk how Coca Cola was made and how in Maharashtra roti and rice were eaten together, he could tell from the sound of her voice that the pain must be driving her to bite her lips and clench her fists.

Deshmukh had not had a chance to have a word with the general manager, but he knew he had to somehow get his word across about Harishankar's hunger strike. When the general manager was about to get into his car after seeing off the tax officer and his wife, Deshmukh, left with no other option, ran up to him. 'Sir, there's something I wanted to say.'

'What about?'

'Harishankar's hunger strike.'

The general manager looked around a little, as if on his guard. 'Well, I've already told you the matter falls under your jurisdiction. How you handle these things is pretty much your own responsibility.'

Deshmukh responded very humbly. 'I wanted your suggestion, sir.'

The general manager was just climbing into his car but stopped short. He put his hand on Deshmukh's back. 'I suggest you persuade Harishankar to call off his hunger strike. But how you do that is your call. Whatever good or bad comes from it will fall on you, not me. Why aren't you taking the help of your subordinate officers in this matter, if I may ask? Some of them are competent people. Get them to help you. Don't worry at all. Nothing's impossible in this world.'

The general manager left, leaving Deshmukh to himself. Deshmukh realized the other deputy chief mining engineers were keeping their distance. They had sat with him for a long time, but not even once had they asked about the workers' unrest in Tarbahar Colliery. They had not tried to find out how he was dealing with that. On the contrary, their eyes and faces bore silent sly smiles, as if they were deriving pleasure from Deshmukh's plight.

All that was yesterday. Sleep eluded Deshmukh. All night he tossed and turned in bed. The thought of whom to consult and about what troubled him deeply. In the morning he called the personnel officer and asked for his opinion.

'In my opinion, sir', said the personnel officer, 'the situation now is such that a truce with Harishankar Babu and his group seems necessary. It would be better to meet their demands.'

'You're aware of the entire sequence of events and yet you still say that? You have seen how fierce the backlash was when the group led by Harishankar Babu was allowed to sign up members. You know that Dhruba Khatua, despite the fact he lacks moral fibre, has the ability to make or break things. And some influence too. As for Harishankar Babu, does he really have the people behind him?'

Traces of a smile broke on the personnel officer's lips. He spoke with humility. 'Sir, we'll do as you say, but I have fourteen or fifteen years of experience in this field. I have been closely observing the masses, the general public, and the trade union. The fact of the matter is that it's not possible to be certain how people will react. Suppose Harishankar Babu comes to some harm; neither the masses nor the government will spare you. That's because he's been sitting on a hunger strike in front of your office.'

'But that's pure and simple blackmail.'

The personnel officer smiled again. 'Wasn't Dhruba Khatua's strike also an attempt at blackmail? If you look at the purpose of trade unions and at the way they conduct themselves, you'll realize their entire political action is based on blackmail. They need to be blackmailed in turn if management wants to escape their grasp.'

Deshmukh found this world very strange. Until now his surroundings had been completely different. Not that he had not been confronted with politics, small time leaders, and touts before. He understood the extent to which the caste system still played a role in politics. He knew that modern political leaders still had a feudal mindset. He was even aware of that most hated phenomenon, fascism. But until now he had believed that things were transparent and straightforward, that two and two added up to four. Never in his past had he come across as aberrant and unthinkable an approach to politics as this. Here two plus two could add up to five or six or seven or eight.

When Deshmukh was studying mining engineering, had it ever crossed his mind he would have to deal with such an absurd system, lacking the most basic of principles? Had the left-leaning Deshmukh of that time realized the true face of the general public and their saviours in this country?

The personnel officer continued. 'Sir, the chair you're occupying isn't just a chair. It's your chariot on this battlefield of the colliery. As long as you hold this job you'll have to fight—with your subordinates, with your superiors, with the workers, and with the officers. At all times you'll have to tread very carefully, looking in all directions. Any misstep can bring you defeat and cause your citadel to crumble. How you fight is, of course, up to you, but I've thought of a way, sir, and you may try it. Among the many demands of the group led by Harishankar Babu is that their union be recognized as legitimate. What I would suggest is that you sidestep this central demand and go ahead and meet the rest of them. I have a feeling they'll accept the decision if they're promised this demand will receive due consideration by management in the future. A member of their group, whose name is Agani Hota, is a key player. If we can satisfy him, I think he'll be able to persuade Harishankar Babu to call off his hunger strike. Agani has a nephew, sir. He's a Brahmin but has been enrolled in the colliery service under the name of Samaru Khadia. This is a case of impersonation. If we give this fellow back his name, Agani will probably come round to accepting our terms.'

'If we tell them we'll consider their demand in the future then they'll go ahead and recruit members, standing near the main counter, and Dhruba Khatua and his group will retaliate.'

'No, sir, not this time. There won't be any opposition from them at all.'

How could the personnel officer say this so confidently? Deshmukh looked him in the eye. The man had on his face an all-knowing smile. 'Dhruba Khatua and his group know their limits. We may have backed down on cutting one week of the workers' pay, but they were not paid for the three days they were on strike, based on the rule that they don't get paid if they don't work. Dhruba Khatua knows the workers won't support a call for another strike so soon. Yes, he and his group will create an uproar, but there's a way to silence them. Two or three people from his circle have been suspended recently on suspicion of stealing. They have a connection with the coal mafia. If we revoke their suspension and reinstate their jobs, I think we can get a grip on Dhruba Khatua.'

The conversation had taken place that morning, and Deshmukh realized he had to take the risk. He had no other option than to agree with the personnel officer. And so he had said yes.

A scream from Anita, strapped into her traction, brought Deshmukh back to his senses. It had been going on for twenty minutes instead of fifteen, as prescribed. It was time to release her. He untied the knot and asked, 'Has the pain gone down? Are you able to move your neck?'

Anita made an indistinct sound. Deshmukh held her, helping her get up. 'Please go and lie down. We'll go to Nagpur soon to see the doctor.'

'How can you go now? There's unrest among the workers in the coal mines.'

'Harishankar Patnaik's hunger strike will perhaps be called off in a day or two. We'll get to know tonight.'

The servant boy came in just then and announced, 'The personnel officer has come.'

'Alone?'

'With two other people.'

'Go and have them sit down in the drawing room. I'll be with them presently.'

In his haste, Deshmukh did not have time to change into something more formal. He left in a rush, leaving Anita sitting on the bed. The personnel officer was accompanied by Agani and a young man. They greeted him. Deshmukh asked them to take a seat.

'I have held preliminary talks', said the personnel officer. 'They've agreed to our terms. Things will be finalized after discussing with you.'

Deshmukh breathed a sigh of relief. It was as if a load was taken off his shoulders. He felt very light. He stretched his hand towards Agani. While clasping Agani's hand, however, he drew back and hung his head. It was this very man he had insulted and expelled from his office the other day, and today he was holding the same man's hand firmly in jubilation. It was as if Deshmukh's personality was dissolving like water. This man, this Agani, must realize the face Deshmukh sahib showed in the office was a mask, not his real face. The personnel officer must have understood how cowardly Deshmukh truly was. He felt deeply humiliated. He could not lift his head to look at them. 'Please sit down. Why have you remained standing?' he asked.

FIFTEEN

The person who asked them to sit down was none other than Deshmukh sahib. Pradyumna could feel his feet shivering. Out of fear, excitement, or weakness? Pradyumna had heard Deshmukh sahib had become stern and pitiless. He was said to have been quite innocent and meek before assuming the position of deputy chief mining engineer, but he had apparently changed completely after that. Even other managers and section heads in the colliery became worried when his name was mentioned. Whenever he happened to come across anyone he would stare at them so intensely they would find it difficult to retain their composure. He was said to have spies everywhere in the colliery; news from every corner made its way to him. After he assumed his new charge the rules and regulations in the office completely changed. The clerks who were used to loitering or drinking tea in the market near the office or in the post office nearby were no longer to be seen. The junior managers who earlier had not gone down into the pit now lacked the courage to stay behind. Earlier the timbermen and dressers would leave for home two to three hours before the end of office hours;

now everyone stayed in the office or in the mine for a full eight hours. The mining sardars were themselves lighting the dynamite fuses. Pradyumna knew of many such changes that had come about within a short period of time. Today that same brutal Deshmukh sahib was greeting them and asking them to be seated.

Pradyumna was feeling very weak. While on the hunger strike, he had only sipped water. Uncle Agani and Harishankar Babu had agreed he could do this. In the beginning, he had been nervous at the thought of going on a hunger strike, especially when his uncle had told him it had been decided at the union meeting that he and Pradyumna would go on a strike. His aunt had created a scene, and Runu and Jhunu had raised their voices in protest, to add to the noise. But that had not changed anything. So his aunt and the two girls had fed Pradyumna and Uncle Agani huge quantities of rice at four in the morning, well before the fast was set to begin.

In his village Pradyumna had been a very different sort of eater; never eating very much, and without any order or system. He would eat a pot of curry or ladoos made of grated sweet coconut or a handful of snacks on the go. If these weren't available, he would gulp down half a pot of pakhal. He always left more than he ate.

Pradyumna's eating habits were a source of friction between him and his sister-in-law; she disapproved of his repeatedly asking for food. His sisters complained about her habit of giving more food to some and less to others. At times his sisters would serve him, and if no one was around he would help himself in the kitchen. His mother, obsessed with ritual purification, suffered no one to enter the cooking room, located in the sacred ishana—the north-eastern corner, dedicated to Lord Shiva. She would, however, spare Pradyumna out of her love for him.

It was this same Pradyumna who had sat on a hunger strike in front of the general office of Tarbahar colliery. At first, he had felt nervous. Would he be able to stave off hunger? Would he pass out? What if he died? For the first time Pradyumna had realized that life was dear to him. He had not experienced so many things. There were many still to be known, many joys and sorrows yet to be experienced. Would he lay down his life out of idealism, for his union?

His uncle had called him aside and spoken in confidence. 'Son, the reason I forced you to take part in the hunger strike was simply because I want you to become an important figure in the colliery. Once the strike is underway, management will want to make a deal with us. That will be the moment to make it aware of your problems and demands, even if nothing else comes of the strike. The second thing is, after you've been on a hunger strike you'll emerge as a leader. Even if management ignores your main demands one thing at least is certain—you'll not have to load tubs anymore.'

His uncle's foresight and the brilliance of his strategy took Pradyumna by surprise. Earlier he had observed Agani Hota in his village from a distance. Sociable and talkative by nature, the Agani Hota of his memory used to stammer and swallow half his words. There was a certain softness to his personality. From the outside he did not seem stern at all. His reputation in the colliery was bad because he kept a concubine from Chhattisgarh and also because he was a heavy drinker. What really gave him a bad name, though, was that he was henpecked by his shrewish wife and had two aggressive daughters, whose morals the people of the colliery suspected. The world of politics acquainted Pradyumna with a different Agani uncle, a man who surprisingly did not stammer while delivering speeches, a man who was firm in his decisions, and whose foresight was appreciated by a person as wise as Harishankar Babu.

Following his uncle's advice Pradyumna had promptly gone on the hunger strike. On the first day, he was surprised to discover he did not feel hungry. On the second day, there were some pangs of hunger but he was able to tolerate them. Then on the third, fourth, and fifth day, he felt no hunger at all. He was able to live without sustenance; this surprised him greatly. The only thing that worried him was that he might become bored and physically weak. He devoured whatever reading materials were at hand: newspapers old and new, books, even the standing orders of Tarbahar colliery and the constitution of the Coal Workers Organization. The fiery speeches by Uncle Agani, which at first had been lapped up eagerly by the enthusiastic crowd that assembled before each new shift, were gradually losing their attraction. His uncle was becoming weak and powerless. Pradyumna felt nothing but exhausted. If anything bothered him, it was being stuck in one place. In the beginning he would chat with Harishankar Babu and his uncle or with the people

who came to stand guard. Later, he got tired of such talk.
The afternoons were particularly difficult on account of the
sun and the heat. He went to sleep at seven in the evening
and woke up at two in the morning.

Deshmukh sahib grabbed his uncle's hands in a display
of great warmth. 'Please sit down, please be seated', he said.

Pradyumna sat on the sofa with the personnel officer and
his uncle. The room was partially lit by a low-wattage bulb;
no one thought about switching on a brighter light. Was
it an air cooler or an air conditioner that could be heard?
Pradyumna was not able to make out which one it was, but
a cool breeze circulated across the room. Pradyumna was
covered in sweat. He missed not having a handkerchief.

All this had happened a short while ago. Uncle Agani
and Pradyumna had gone to Deshmukh sahib's house,
accompanied by the personnel officer who had come to
fetch them. It was in that room that Deshmukh sahib had
firmly grasped his uncle's hand. 'Sir', said Uncle Agani.
'We're well aware of the difficulties you face, and we'll
never cause you any problems. Our aim is not to force you
to recognize our union and break off all ties with Dhruba
Khatua's. We know how to assert ourselves. We have
only one demand—allow us to fight our own fight. Let
management remain neutral.'

When the personnel officer had come to get them,
Harishankar Babu had remarked, 'Why hasn't Deshmukh
sahib come to us? Why should we go to him?'

Agani uncle had, however, been happy. He had tried
to reason with Harishankar Babu. 'See, management is

management, and sahibs are sahibs. Management has already shown itself to be flexible. It would be stupid of us not to take advantage of this opportunity.'

Harishankar Babu said nothing more, preferring to lapse into a tomb-like silence. Uncle Agani went to meet Deshmukh sahib against Harishankar Babu's wishes and took Pradyumna along. Before going he whispered to Pradyumna, 'Harishankar Babu never could be practical. That's why he hasn't risen in politics.' At the house the sahib told Uncle Agani, 'Look, management has no position on the union, but two things are important for us. One is production, and the other is peace and discipline. If these are disrupted, we have to step in.'

His uncle answered. 'There's no way production will be disrupted; we can guarantee that from now on. Yes, production was brought to a standstill earlier, but that was Dhruba Khatua's doing. As for peace and discipline, we are absolute Gandhians, sir. Why else would we have decided to go on a hunger strike? We would perhaps have started breaking and smashing things.'

In the meantime, someone brought in four cups of tea along with glasses of cold water. There was a plate full of biscuits and sweets. Pradyumna reached out and bit into a biscuit without thinking. The very moment he did that he remembered he was on a hunger strike. He had not eaten for the past three days, only drinking water. He was overcome by a sense of shame at the signal this act might possibly send. What could he do now? He was able neither to chew the biscuit nor raise his head to look at either Deshmukh sahib or the personnel officer. His ears turned red.

'We have two demands that need to be met before we can have a formal discussion', his uncle had said. 'These, you have to accept. They're not big demands, and you have the power to grant them.' Uncle Agani kept quiet for a while. Deshmukh sahib and the personnel officer looked at him questioningly. Pradyumna had a piece of biscuit concealed in his fist, as if it was his secret sin. The piece he had bitten off had got stuck in his mouth, as if it was an insult. He could neither swallow nor raise his head. Maybe Deshmukh sahib was laughing at him, finding Pradyumna's predicament amusing and not listening to what Uncle Agani was saying. Perhaps he was thinking what a fraud Pradyumna was and how he was cheating by pretending to be on a hunger strike.

His uncle continued. 'The first of our demands relates to Om Prakash, who broke his leg in the brawl. He has no sick leave in his account, and we want him placed in a job that's not too demanding. The second has to do with Pradyumna, my nephew. He works in this colliery under the name of Samaru Khadia. He should be shifted to the office as a clerk and, when his name has been changed through an affidavit, he should appear in the records not as Samaru Khadia but as Pradyumna Mishra.'

Pradyumna's ears pricked up. His heart beat faster. What would Deshmukh sahib say? He raised his head and looked. This was the moment his identity, his being, his future, and his life would be restored to him. How his future would play out would be discovered in a moment. He would learn the fate of his successes and failures, his laughter and happiness. Pradyumna knew what Deshmukh sahib would say before he actually said it. The piece of biscuit stuck in his mouth slid down his throat before he could stop it.

Pradyumna had had no idea all his problems would be solved so soon. When Deshmukh sahib answered 'yes', it was as if a bell tolled in a distance. Pradyumna closed his eyes in happiness and imagined a seashore spreading from horizon to horizon. A limitless expanse, devoid of human presence. Without tourists, peddlers selling shells, boys hawking puffed rice, camera-toting travellers. There were not even the seaside dwellers, the nulias, who make their living from the sea. From a long way off a small point was advancing, increasing in size as it moved forward, taking on form. Oh, it was Minakshi! The woman coming towards him was Minakshi. Agitation was sweeping over the lonely seashore. The deathly silence and solitary emptiness was becoming even emptier and lonelier because of her. Oh, Minakshi! Alas! Why did Pradyumna have to think of Minakshi now?

Deshmukh sahib shut his eyes for a minute. 'Alright', he said. 'Agreed. You may consider these two conditions met. We can draw up the formal agreement later on, but first you all should call off your hunger strike.'

'The strike will be called off', answered Uncle Agani. 'But then we should let Harishankar Babu know what has transpired between us. Our party members also ought to know this. Why not do this—come tomorrow morning

at ten o'clock and give Harishankar Babu some fruit juice
to drink. After that we'll make the formal announcement
there . . .'

Deshmukh sahib cut him short. 'Remember one thing—
no matter how much political mileage you might be getting
from this hunger strike, management does not like to be
held up to ridicule. Please don't make any announcement
that will further upset Dhruba Khatua's group.'

His uncle's humble demeanour surprised Pradyumna.
Just a few days ago Deshmukh sahib had turned him out of
his office unceremoniously. How could he now try so hard
to ingratiate himself? Pradyumna himself would not have
acted so obsequiously. Agani said, 'Rest assured, sir. We
won't do anything to inconvenience you.'

Pradyumna left the house with the others. The world
seemed beautiful and bewitching to him, despite the
sweltering summer night. The Tarbahar coal mine, which
had never brought him happiness or peace, had taken
on a new look. Seductive. The layer of dust smothering
his existence had disappeared. His days of monotonous
incarceration were at an end.

When he got into the jeep after taking leave of
Deshmukh sahib and the personnel officer, his uncle said,
'Pradyumna, go and tell the other committee members the
hunger strike will be called off tomorrow. There'll be a
procession once this has been formally announced, with
Deshmukh sahib giving some fruit juice to Netaji. Bring
everyone to the strike venue; there'll be a discussion. Also,
go home and give your aunt and the others the news. Before

we began the strike she had told me we were out of flour. I don't know how they've managed. They must have missed out on their mutton on Sunday and your aunt must be in a rage. Go and talk to her nicely, will you?'

Beneath his uncle's outward appearance of hardness and practicality lurked a tender heart; Pradyumna could see that today. How many different kinds of men can exist within one man? Pradyumna had a lot more to learn! He was slowly being won over by his uncle's personality.

The jeep dropped him off near his uncle's house. For the past three days Pradyumna had not stirred from where he had been on his fast. It seemed to him as if the colony had been washed clean by a fresh shower of rain. The colony, well known to him, seemed radiant in new attire. Pradyumna could see the light was on in the house.

He had thought their hunger strike would have plunged the entire house into sepulchral silence, that his aunt would have been asleep in her darkened room, that Runu and Jhunu would have reduced their conversation to a bare minimum, that the entire house would have fallen intolerably quiet. But nothing of the sort seemed to have happened. The house resonated with activity and the buzz of conversation. The moment he set foot in the house Pradyumna knew a card game was going on in the bedroom. Hearing Pradyumna's footsteps, Jhunu came running out. Catching sight of him, she reacted in surprise, 'Oh, my, is that you? Mother, Bhaina's here.'

She took Pradyumna into the bedroom, dragging him by the hand. There his aunt, Runu, and Peter were sitting on the cot playing a card game. Smiling, his aunt asked, 'I thought you were on a death fast; how can you be here?'

Peter never spoke to Pradyumna. He sat with his head down shuffling the deck of cards. Runu sat bashfully, her face turned away. She had never felt at ease with Pradyumna. Jhunu held his hand and stroked his cheek and jaw, as if she was close to him. 'Mother', she asked. 'Do you see how thin Bhaina has become after only three days?' Suddenly Pradyumna was reminded of Minakshi. Would she really be waiting for him? Even if she was, did Pradyumna have the courage to marry a Khandayat girl? Pradyumna had seemingly found his own ground to stand upon after a long time. Soon, he would be freed from his identity as Samaru Khadia and be able to define himself, rediscover the glory of his family tradition, his past, and his memory. But would he really be able to find himself even after he changed back from Samaru Khadia to Pradyumna? Would he ever be happy without Minakshi? Would he be fulfilled? Perhaps Pradyumna was not destined for completeness, perhaps he would always remain only half-made.

A secret resolution had been made in his mind: he would no longer accept the situation in his uncle's house, or in this coal mine. He knew he would suffocate here. He would cut himself loose and live his life on his own terms. No, he did not need to play the role of Samaru Khadia anymore. Hereafter he would be Pradyumna Mishra, the real Pradyumna Mishra.

SIXTEEN

Where were the others? Harishankar opened his eyes and looked around. Dawn had broken; the sun was up. The morning vendors—the milkman, the bread seller, the newspaper boy—were up and about. The school bus drove past with its load of students. A hay-laden bullock cart crossed in front of the pandal at a crawl. Two or three people went by on their bicycles. One got down and greeted Harishankar. Today was the fourth day of the strike, but Agani and the others had left. Harishankar knew from the way they had spoken yesterday they would not be back.

How quickly everything can change! Just a few days ago Agani had decided to form a new union, chosen Harishankar as its leader, heaped praise on him at meetings and functions, and took strong offence if anyone spoke ill of him. That very same Agani, who had forced him to go on a hunger strike, had left him on his own almost since it started.

Perhaps that was all Harishankar's fault; perhaps Agani was right. He was a practical man, after all, and had to be right. Harishankar was a dreamer, and probably also too emotional. No matter what Harishankar thought, there really was no place for ideals in this world. When he had first come into union politics, Hema Babu was a young leader and Harishankar his most devoted follower. The idealism he had cherished, the romanticized image of socialism he had been attracted to and yet had only a vague notion of was gone. The union for him meant taking on the world. Yet what had all that come to today? It had been turned into a business from which its leaders could profit. Harishankar was tired of this scramble and stampede for monetary gain. He could not do it anymore. No, he couldn't.

Last night the personnel officer had called Agani away; later, Agani had come back from his meeting with Deshmukh. He had returned, puffed up with the pride of victory. 'Our work is done, Netaji.'

By then, Harishankar knew what had happened between Agani and Deshmukh. It was all very predictable, he thought—almost predetermined—that it should have happened like that. It seemed to him that even before the strike was called people had somehow known this would be the outcome.

When Agani proposed calling off the strike, adding that Deshmukh sahib would come the following morning and bring some fruit juice before plans were drawn up for the procession and the meeting, Harishankar felt certain of the inevitable. In a voice that was slightly raised, he said, 'I won't end my hunger strike, Agani.'

Agani fell from the sky. 'You won't end it? What are you blabbering about, Netaji? You won't call off the strike even after our demands have been met?'

'How have our demands been met, Agani? They'll be forwarded to a higher authority, that's all. Who is this higher authority? And who can assure us this higher body—whatever it might be—will seriously consider our demands? Who can assure us they'll accept them even if they do agree to consider them? We could have sent our demands to this higher authority without having to resort to a strike.'

'Tell me what else Deshmukh sahib could have done. He doesn't have supreme power.'

'Did you go on strike because of Deshmukh sahib, Agani? Didn't we want recognition for our union? Let me ask what union you wanted to get recognized. In our country is there even one that is not controlled by management? Tell me which union truly represents the people and is driven by the popular will?'

'What can we do, Netaji? We'll have to have a union like all the rest. We'll have to stand up to our competitors.'

Harishankar stared at Agani for a long time. Didn't he remember the days before Independence? Had he forgotten Gandhiji's message, satyagraha, and fasting unto death? Had he forgotten about yearning to do something, about rising above the gross materialistic lust for power and position? 'I don't know whether you still believe in Gandhian values or not', said Harishankar, 'but I do. It seems to me, after

so many days, that if you set them aside there's no other
way to live your life. Tell me if our politics, ridden with
violence, has brought us anything other than slavery.
Slavery to the police, slavery to management, slavery to
crooks and rogues. Where has the talk about awakening
the people's conscience gone? What has happened to the
idea of a mass movement?'

Agani laughed. 'Netaji, you're proposing Gandhian
values at a time when Gandhi has been relegated to the
history books. Okay, since you mentioned Gandhiji,
please think about this. Was Nehru, Gandhiji's most
ardent follower, Gandhian in thought, consciousness, and
action? And didn't Gandhiji contradict himself at every
step? Besides, didn't the story about his sexual perversion,
especially his sleeping with a young woman during the
communal riot in Nuakhali, cause communist leaders to
raise a hue and cry. Did Gandhiji himself contradict the
story? Or did anyone else, on his behalf? Did Nehru or
the Congress party? Idealism is like that. It is said Gautam
Buddha ate the flesh of swine towards the end of his
life. History bears witness to this: all idealism ends up
contradicting its own philosophical premises.

Harishankar was at a loss for words; he never was very
good at arguing. It is true Gandhiji and Gandhian values
had always had their detractors. Nor was Harishankar that
convinced about Gandhian philosophy. Until recently
Hema Babu had been his ideal, the same Hema Babu who
was a Gandhian in name only, someone who had never
acted on Gandhian principles. But now it seemed to him

that Gandhianism was the most valued path; there was no other way to proceed. He believed in that firmly. A strong moral force was taking control of Harishankar, forcing him not to call off his strike.

Harishankar said nothing and lay down quietly. The committee members of the union crowded around him. Harishankar lay there with his eyes shut, feeling weak. His mouth was parched; his lips were cracking. For the first couple of days Harishankar had felt hungry and thirsty, but now he was no longer troubled by either. It was as if he had long ago forgotten the need to eat. He felt as if he had reserves of food and undying energy. On those, he could survive for many days.

Harishankar could hear Agani calling 'Netaji, Netaji.' His words seemed to be coming from far away. He did not feel like opening his eyes. What was left for him to say, anyway? He did not know how to argue; he would not be able to cope with rhetoric cleverly deployed. He was fine with what he had understood. His body was being drained of energy, as if a dark cloud was bearing down on him. His tongue was getting sucked back into his throat. No, he had to prepare, he had to fight. Enough was enough; no more. His life so far had been in vain. What need did he have for power or riches now? Life had to have a purpose.

What would Harishankar do if he did not end the hunger strike? Was the strike for his own benefit? What did he want? Harishankar did not know. Yes, that certainly was true, and during the strike he would think about his motives. He would discover the purpose of

the fast while it was still underway. Maybe the reason
for it was to purify himself, to express grief and remorse
for all that he had had to do in the name of the union.
Maybe it was to awaken the people, to change their way
of thinking. Their moral consciousness had degenerated
to such an extent even unethical acts could be cloaked
in legitimacy. Maybe his fast was against this decadence.
Harishankar did not know for sure. Was he confused?
He did not know. Perhaps, but maybe not. Perhaps he
was still a novice. There was still a lot for him to know,
to learn. Perhaps, from this day forward, his approach to
politics would change.

Harishankar lay asleep with his eyes closed, not
responding to Agani's call. He felt weak. For two or three
nights he had not slept well, bitten by mosquitoes and
kept awake by the noisy throngs. His eyelids felt heavy.
He did not know when he lapsed into sleep. Suddenly it
was broken; he looked around and saw no one. The place
was empty. What was the time? Had Harishankar been
asleep for a while? So, Agani and his friends had ended the
strike. Neither Mitrabhanu nor Chandrasekhar, from the
production and workshop sections, were there. The people
who came to keep watch at night had also left. All of them
were gone, leaving Harishankar behind.

He felt very helpless. And afraid. As if a scorching
desert stretched out in front of him and the caravan he was
travelling in had vanished, leaving him stranded. Wherever
he looked he saw only a boundless expanse of barren land,
with him standing alone in its middle.

It was a moonlit night. In some far-off place a band of people from Gorakhpur were singing devotional songs. Their bhajans had a strange appeal. Harishankar got up on his feet; he felt restless. What could he do? Flee? But if he did, would he be able to look anybody in the face tomorrow? On the other hand, could he run the union on his own? A single man with no union members to back him up. With no masses or workers supporting him? What would he gain by pressing on with the strike? Tomorrow the entire colliery would be awash with the news Harishankar Patnaik had gone mad. People would come to look at him like an animal in a zoo. They would look at him and snigger.

Harishankar had thought that the union had his back, that he could count on the support of at least thirty members. He had thought that he would be able to continue the struggle with the help of these thirty people, that he could influence people and make them think about union politics and the moral decadence weighing them down. Maybe that was his mistake. Now, he clearly understood that no one had given him the right to claim the union as his own, that he was merely the expendable medium through which the struggle took place.

Would he get up and leave? Would he go and tell Agani, 'Whatever had to happen has happened; I am with you.' After that he could abandon the union and sit quietly at home, looking after his family, his troubled wife, his old mother, and his sons, who were going astray. He could do his job from ten to five and distance himself from everything in Tarbahar Colliery.

Hadn't it been enough for Harishankar to distance himself from Hema Babu, forget about politics, and rear his fawn? What had suddenly come over him? Why had he re-entered union politics? Had he done that for power? For status? For money and respect? True, for a long time Harishankar had been thinking about doing something. But should that have been forming the union? The politics of violence? Was there any point to forming a union that would do management's bidding? Apart from cheating people, covering for management, and making some money, what benefit would come of this, for the country and its people?

The people understand everything. They do not trust political leaders anymore. They no longer support the leaders of unions. Sometimes, they are even afraid of these people. At others, they make a display of their humility and support only for their own personal gain. Harishankar had intended to form a new union completely backed by the people. He wanted to show how flawed and fleeting Hema Babu's notions were about the general public, the masses. Maybe they had forgotten their own identity, their own values. As Agani said, Gandhiji was now safely ensconced in the pages of history, his non-violence and satyagraha rendered obsolete. The masses require strict administration. The Emergency. Our country tends towards a lack of discipline. Otherwise, there would have been no need to impose the Emergency for the trains to run on time. Otherwise, milkmen would not think it was okay to dilute their milk with water. Otherwise, people unwilling to take bribes would not be considered pure idealists.

The constable on the night beat came up to Harishankar. From the first day of the strike he had been sent there by the police to protect the strikers. He came close and asked where the others were and why they had left Netaji alone.

Harishankar did not reply. He asked him to sit. 'I need to ask you a few things. Tell me, have you ever given much thought to the public in general?'

The constable laughed. 'To tell you the truth', he answered, 'our work, like yours, is connected with the people, the masses. It's surprising your ideas about them and ours are quite similar. The masses take it for granted that the police and politicians are both on the take, that they're both liars and are both ready to sell themselves to the administration and to power.'

'Okay, so that's what the masses think of you and us. Tell me now how you view them.'

'To be honest, I haven't been able to form a clear idea. Think of this. The people who loot and set fires during communal riots are the very same ones who form peace committees and processions, making allegations that the police are unable to maintain peace and order. Tell me, which of these is the real face of the masses? Which would you want to choose? Maybe the masses are directionless, and like sheep they'll go whichever way you pull them. Maybe the masses don't have the power to think, the power to discriminate. They're like a stream of water.'

Was this Hema Babu all over again? The same perspective, the same attitude? But then Hema Babu was right. There is no need to trouble oneself about the masses.

Harishankar knew he could not protest or argue but only say the masses are not this or should not act like that. He had no idea how to change their ideas, habits, tendencies. Perhaps going on a strike was correct. Perhaps many more people had to throw themselves into the movement. But not today. One day, of course, things could change. The masses would be able to transform themselves. A time would come when this reckoning would happen, when people would recognize their values, their sense of ethics. Until then, someone somewhere ought to keep the strike going. That is how the great movement for satyagraha would commence.

Why should Harishankar bother about what one person did and another did not. Did he even have to worry about what his strike would accomplish? Maybe it would all be for nothing. Was Gandhiji's fast able to prevent riots or the partition of India? Many more Gandhis should have come forward after Gandhiji. Harishankar lay back down on the cloth mat and straightened out his back.

'Where have the others gone, Netaji?' asked the constable.

'Most likely they won't continue with the strike.'

'Why not?'

'They've got what they wanted.'

'And you?' The constable felt at a loss. Harishankar kept silent. He shut his eyes. Shouldn't he say something? Wasn't this constable also a part of the masses? Wouldn't it be important to explain to him why Harishankar did not want to break his fast? But Harishankar kept quiet. Wasn't he distancing himself from the people, from the masses? Should he, who had set out to wage a battle for them, cut himself off like this?

Harishankar remained silent. He did not feel like speaking. So much talk and heated debate, so many illustrations; it was all exhausting! He could no longer speak. He would never be able to express in words what he felt in his heart. He kept quiet. He went back to lying on the cloth mat, his feet apart, his hands crossed and supporting his head, his eyes shut. He remained flat on his back, ignoring the questions of the constable.

After a while the constable said, 'Well, stay lying down, Netaji. I'm off on my rounds.'

He left, never to return that night. Harishankar lay there alone, enduring the bites of mosquitoes. He remained wide awake. The Gorakhpuri bhajan from far off had stopped. The moon had disappeared. Surrounded by the sounds of trains rattling past, dogs barking, the whistle of the Nepali watchman, the crickets singing, he spent the entire night gazing at the stars in the sky.

The morning had advanced quite a bit. The sun was up. Harishankar's throat felt parched. Would he end the strike? When a large number of supporters were with him he had not felt the pangs of thirst and hunger. Once alone, the strike became unbearable. Harishankar could not decide whether to end it. His thoughts were muddled, straying from Agani to Hema Babu to Dhruba Khatua. While thinking of Hema Babu, his mind took him to his father, with his matted hair and attire of a sanyasi. He was unable to open his eyes and look around, but he had not slept. His entire life, from past to present, flashed before his eyes.

The main road in his village on a dusky evening. Harishankar is looking at a bearded man—his father—who is telling him: 'I'm sure you'll understand me when you grow up. When you do, I trust you'll forgive me. I never meant do wrong to your mother. Try to make her happy.'

Leaving Harishankar alone by the side of the road at twilight, a sanyasi is wading deeper into the village fields and Harishankar is standing alone, all alone. Someone taps on his shoulder. Harishankar turns around. Dhruba Khatua. He is smiling, saying, 'So you've had your fill of fun with the union, Netaji?'

The face of Dhruba Khatua fades into Hema Babu's. The compulsive paan-chewer and ever-inebriated Hema Babu is saying, 'I don't give a damn for your masses. The masses, my foot.'

Harishankar presses on, pedalling his bicycle. Where is he going? He has to reach the general manager's office quickly. It is already eleven o'clock. That Ghosh Babu always tries to taunt him. Harishankar's mother is running after him. 'Hari, Haria, dear boy Harishankar. Leave me some paisa. There's no paddy in the house. I want to eat vada and samosa. Don't you remember I pawned my jewellery to give you twenty rupees before you left to get a job?'

'Netaji, Netaji!'

Was Harishankar dreaming? He was not asleep; he had merely closed his eyes. Somebody shouted, and he opened them. Aah, it was so painful to do that. Was the earth spinning like a top? With great difficulty Harishankar looked up and realized it was the person who had lent them the mike. He was saying, 'I'm taking this away, Netaji.'

Harishankar did not reply; he shut his eyes again. Next, the person from the tent house would come and take away the tent. The pandal would be empty, deserted. Harishankar would lie under the open sky. The people of Tarbahar Colliery would stand in a circle around him, laughing. They would all be laughing out loud. Never before would they have seen such an amusing sight.

Harishankar began to lose his focus once again. Which town was this? So many people, such a throng. Was this a meeting someone had called? Or was it the Rath Yatra? Where were they headed in such large numbers? Out of that sea of humanity a mendicant was reaching out to him. 'Hari, son Harishankar. I went to the Kumbh Mela. Good that we have been able to meet. I often think of you. I haven't been able to do right by you, son.'

Harishankar stretched out his hand, but could not reach the one extended towards him. Where had the hand of the mendicant gone? Where was the mendicant? Harishankar was caught up in the stream of the surging crowd, moving forward. Where was he going? Had he come somewhere? Was he being lifted off his feet by someone? Was someone swooping down upon him like a vulture? No, the person pulling him up was Deshmukh sahib. He was saying, 'Please come, Netaji. Mr Mirchandani is in the helicopter.' Harishankar looked up. Yes, there was a helicopter up in the sky. Ghosh Babu was near the door, leaning half out. Deshmukh sahib was suspended from a rope hanging from the helicopter. He lifted Harishankar up. There were people below. People all around. It was the Kumbh Mela. He had once seen such a throng in Puri during the Rath Yatra. He thought he spotted Ferguson sahib in the crowd, in cap and shorts, blowing his whistle. Ghosh Babu was shouting from the helicopter, 'You're late even today, Netaji?'

Who had snatched Harishankar away from this scene? Harishankar looked about, his eyes wide open. Was that Om Prakash? Yes, it was. Did Harishankar try to say something? He was feeling very thirsty. His tongue was thickening. No, he would not drink a drop of water. He would press on with his fast. His fast unto death. He would not sip a drop; he would not end his fast. Not ever.

'Are you not feeling well, Netaji?' asked Om Prakash.

Harishankar could not hear him clearly anymore, as if his words were floating in from far away. If everyone had gone, leaving him, what had brought Om Prakash back? Was he here to take away the tent?

Om Prakash spoke close to Harishankar's ear. 'They might desert you, Netaji, but I can't. You're our leader. You should have patience. We'll form a new union. I believe the people of Tarbahar Colliery will support our union.'

Harishankar shut his eyes. Aah, such peace! Om Prakash was with him. He was not alone. He had at least one person to support him. It seemed to him he was standing at one end of the village at twilight, dressed as a sanyasi, with a flowing beard. He was telling Om Prakash, 'You'll know what I meant when you grow up. When you do, don't call me impractical and blame me.'

As he said this, he was wading deep into the village fields, leaving Om Prakash stranded at the end of the village. Suddenly Harishankar was flooded with a sense of peace. He no longer felt agitated or disturbed. Peace, such peace! Where were so many people headed? Oh, my God, this was an enormous rally, with Harishankar in the lead. Harishankar turned around to see the huge crowd following him. The entire population of Tarbahar colliery was present. Harishankar had never before seen a procession as large. Harishankar could clearly pick out Hema Babu, Dhruba Khatua, Agani. Even Deshmukh, Ferguson sahib, and Mr Mirchandani were there. Aah, with what zest the little children were marching, just as they did during school parades! How enthusiastic the children were! It seemed as if someone was chanting 'Ram Dhun', the song dearest to Harishankar. The recording of that song had long been unavailable. Who had found it?

Just as Harishankar was heaving a sigh of relief, he remembered Om Prakash. Where was he? How was he able to walk in the procession with his broken leg in a thick plaster cast? Where was he now? Harishankar tried to shout 'Om Prakash, Om Prakash, where are you?'

His shout was drowned out by the din of the crowd. Where was Om Prakash? No one answered. Harishankar cried out, 'Stop. Please stop the procession. Tell me where Om Prakash is.'

The surging crowd pushed him onward. Harishankar was at the vanguard of the procession, but he was losing control.

He was being shoved forward by the crowd. Someone was playing 'Ram Dhun' at full volume. Harishankar's words were lost under the harsh grating sound of the recording. Harishankar kept advancing, propelled by the crowd. The assembled voices shouted the victory chant.

Deshmukh sahib and the doctor were bent over Harishankar. The venue of the fast was buzzing and crawling with people. Two or three jeeps stood at a distance. Everyone was speaking in whispers. The police officer-in-charge was making his way forward, navigating through the throng. Deshmukh sahib was saying to the doctor, 'Doctor, the life of this person has to be saved somehow, anyhow.'

The doctor put his blood pressure instrument away and felt Harishankar's pulse once again. His face assumed a grave expression before he spoke. 'I'm doing my best, but there isn't much hope.'

ACKNOWLEDGEMENTS

Apart from the late lamented Jagadish Mohanty, whose earnest wish it was to see his *Nija Nija Panipatha* translated into English during his lifetime, the translators take this opportunity to express their gratitude to the following people for the different ways in which they have inspired this project:

- Sarojini Sahoo, wife of the author and an author in her own right, for helping to give reality to the dream of her husband by giving copyright permission;
- Bhagirathi Mishra, Devidas Mishra, Asit Mohanty, Kedar Mishra and Saroj Bala, for communicating the buzz and hum of the heady Jagadish era they lived through;
- Swarnarenu Mohapatra, who confirmed for us the abiding charm of the novel as well as its deep human significance;
- Anant Mahapatra, J.P. Das, Kamalakanta Mohapatra, Dipti Ranjan Pattanaik and Basant Kumar Tripathy, for keeping faith with us and urging us on;

- Professor Bijay K. Danta, Tezpur University, Dr S. Deepika, Utkal University and Dr Tyagraj Thakur, Silicon Institute of Technology, Sambalpur, for their suggestions on finessing the introduction.

Last but not least, we take this opportunity to say 'thank you' to two people who played a stellar role in the birth of the book: Ananya Bhatia, who kick-started the publication process during her very brief stint at Penguin Random House, and Rea Mukherjee, the present commissioning editor, who saw the work through to its glorious end.

Penguin Random House India's decision to publish the book under their signature imprint of 'Penguin Modern Classics' has immensely served the cause of this novel. For this, we are indebted.